BRANDED IN MEMORY

SILVANA G. SÁNCHEZ

VESELY ACADEMY

Academy of Extraordinary Creatures

The Soul Thief

Curse the Moon

The Blood of Kings

*Be the first to know when Silvana's next book is available!
Follow her on Bookbub to get an alert whenever she has a
new release, preorder, or discount!*

To Gavriil and Luciana,
and to their blissful future.

So I love you because I know no other way than this:
Where I does not exist, nor you,
So close that your hand on my chest is my hand,
So close that your eyes close as I fall asleep.

— PABLO NERUDA

MY FREE AUDIOBOOKS

Do you like FREE audiobooks?

Go check out my YouTube channel!

Subscribe and get notified when new books are up!

Dearest Darklings,

Branded in Memory came to existence because of your many impassioned requests for more of Gavriil and Luciana's love story, following the revelation of their tragic fate in *Runt of the Pack*. I'm pleased to assure you, countless chapters of our beloved couple remain. This is but a glimpse of them.

The following scenes did not make it to *Branded in Love*, the first book in the Bad Boy Shifters of the Unnatural Brethren series. However, you'll find them presented in a sequence that unveils the beautiful tapestry of Gavriil and Luciana's relationship after their romance first bloomed.

The events narrated in *Branded in Memory* take off after Gavriil's fierce confrontation with Cassandra

Deveraux on the night of her branding—as told in the book *Cast in Blood*.

The union of the Deveraux and Alexeev houses is all but imposed on the Ursa King after a year of Luciana's passing... But fate holds a secret hand for our beloved couple. And all will be revealed in the next installment in the Bad Boy Shifters series: *Wings of Shadow*.

For now, it is my sincere wish that the following pages sweep you away from the painful moments our heroes have endured, and deliver you to happier days, days of romance under the Roman sun, and cozy moments by the fireplace in wintry Russian lands.

Embrace the magic, my Darklings, and let Gavriil and Luciana's love story warm your hearts once more.

In love and gratitude,

Silvana.

BRANDED IN MEMORY

A love stolen by fate is forever branded in memory

Gavriil Alexeev, the mighty Ursa King, is a man torn between two worlds. Bound by duty to forge an alliance through marriage, his heart remains unwaveringly faithful to Luciana, the human mate he lost too soon.

As he prepares to bind himself to a witch he doesn't love, Gavriil finds solace and torment in the vivid memories of the woman who forever changed his world.

Torn between the weight of his crown and the longing in his soul, Gavriil must navigate a treacherous path. His clan needs this alliance to survive, but can he truly lead with a broken heart?

Will the echoes of a love so pure give him the strength to face his future, or will they forever chain him to a past he cannot reclaim?

BRANDED IN MEMORY

GAVRIIL ALEXEEV

The patter of rain, incessant against the leaded glass windows of my Parisian study, mirrors the tumultuous thoughts cascading through my mind. I stand before the hearth, one hand braced against the ornate mantelpiece, the other clutching a crystal tumbler of amber liquid. The flames cast dancing shadows across the room, their warmth doing little to thaw the chill that has settled in my bones.

I raise the glass to my lips, savoring the burn of the aged whiskey as it slides down my throat. It's a futile attempt to dull the ache in my chest, to quiet the echoes of Cassandra's angry words still ringing in my ears. The taste reminds me of home, of Saint Petersburg and the life I left behind. A life that seems a lifetime ago, yet the memories remain as fresh as the day I walked away.

My gaze drifts to the portrait above the fireplace —a stern-faced man with familiar dark eyes staring back at me. *Father.* Even now, years after his passing, I feel the weight of his expectations pressing down on my shoulders like a physical burden.

"What would you have done?" I murmur, my voice barely audible above the crackling fire. "How did you balance duty and desire?"

The question hangs unanswered in the air, much like the countless times I've posed it over the years. Father always made it seem so effortless—ruling the clan, maintaining alliances, putting the needs of our people above his own. Did he ever struggle as I do now? Did he ever wish for a different path?

I shake my head, banishing the thought. It doesn't matter now. *I* am the Ursa King, and I must do what is best for my people, regardless of my personal feelings.

My eyes fall on the crumpled paper in the fireplace, the remains of the engagement announcement I'd drafted earlier. The flames lick at its edges, consuming my carefully laid plans. I watch as it turns to ash, a fitting metaphor for the shambles my life has become.

Hours earlier, Deveraux Manor was alive with music and laughter, the air thick with magic as the most powerful supernatural families in the world gathered to celebrate Yule. I close my eyes, remembering the moment Cassandra appeared at the top of the grand staircase. She was breathtaking in her gossamer gown, the crystals catching the light like myriad stars. For a brief moment, I allowed myself to imagine a future where she looked at me with something other than disdain.

The memory of her descent plays out behind my closed eyelids. The way the fabric of her dress shimmered with each step, the subtle sway of her hips, the proud tilt of her chin. She was every inch the Deveraux heiress—powerful, beautiful, and utterly untouchable.

I met her at the bottom of the stairs, offering my hand as was expected. The moment our skin touched, I felt the spark of magic—a promise of the power our union could bring. But beneath that, I sensed her reluctance, her barely concealed anger at being forced into this position.

"Cassandra," I said, my voice low and meant only for her ears. "You look ravishing."

Her eyes flashed, a mix of emotions I couldn't

quite decipher. "Let's get this over with," she replied, her tone clipped.

The rest of the evening was a blur of introductions, political maneuverings, and feigned smiles. I played my part to perfection, the charming and powerful Ursa King, while Cassandra stood by my side, a vision of cold beauty. But beneath the surface, tension simmered, ready to boil over at any moment.

And boil over it did, when the time came for the branding ritual.

I open my eyes, the memory too vivid, too painful to relive in its entirety. My gaze falls on my hands, remembering the feel of Cassandra's skin beneath my fingers as I weaved my magic around her. The branding ceremony—meant to be a moment of connection, of promise—had instead driven the final wedge between us.

"You have no right!" she hissed minutes ago, in this very room, her voice low but filled with venom. "I don't love you, Gavriil. I never will."

I knew, of course. Knew of her love for the vampire Dristan, of the child she carries—a fact that still twists in my gut like a knife. But duty demanded I pressed on, to secure the alliance between our families, to ensure the future of my clan.

"You can't do this, Gavriil!" Cassandra shouted,

her eyes flashing with anger and unshed tears. "You can't just decide my future for me!"

I stood there, impassive on the outside while my heart ached within. "It's already done, Cassandra. The branding is complete. You're my mate now, in the eyes of both our families."

"I don't want to be your mate!" she spat. "I love Dristan. I'm carrying his child, for gods' sake!"

The mention of the vampire's name, of the creature growing within her, struck me like a physical blow. But I steeled myself, keeping my voice level. "That changes nothing. This union is bigger than you and me. It's about the future of our kin."

"*Your* kin," she corrected, her voice cold. "I want no part of this."

And then she stormed out, leaving me alone with the consequences of my actions.

The glass in my hand shatters, shards of crystal embedding themselves in my palm. I barely feel the pain, too lost in my own thoughts. Blood drips onto the expensive Persian rug, staining the intricate patterns. It's a mess—much like my life at this moment.

With a growl of frustration, I move to my desk, pulling out the first aid kit I keep in the bottom drawer. As I clean and bandage the wound, my eyes fall on the framed photograph hidden beneath a stack of papers. My heart clenches as I uncover it, revealing the smiling face of the woman I loved—*still* love.

Luciana.

My fingers trace the curve of her cheek, evoking the warmth of her skin, the sound of her laugh. For a moment, I allow myself to remember—to feel. Her face swims before me, hazel eyes filled with warmth and love. The memory of her presence seems to fill the room, chasing away the shadows.

"My love," I whisper, reaching out as if I could touch her. But my fingers meet only cold glass, and the illusion shatters.

Luciana is gone. A year has passed since I lost her, yet the wound feels as fresh as the day she was taken from me. I press the heels of my hands against my eyes, fighting back the tears that threaten to fall. The bear inside me roars in anguish, longing for its mate.

But I am the Ursa King. I don't have the luxury of wallowing in my sorrow. My people need me—need this union with the Deveraux family. The supernatural world is changing, old alliances shifting like sand beneath our feet. If my clan is to survive, to thrive, I must secure our position.

Even if it means sacrificing my own happiness.

I stand, squaring my shoulders as I face my

father's portrait once more. "I will do what must be done," I say, my voice gaining strength. "For our people. For our future."

Moving back to my desk, I pull out a fresh sheet of paper. With a steady hand, I begin to rewrite the announcement, each word a testament to my resolve. As the Ursa King, I will do my duty—no matter the personal cost.

The words flow from my pen, formal and detached:

"It is with great pleasure that we announce the engagement of His Majesty, Gavriil Alexeev, King of the Ursa Clan, to Lady Cassandra Deveraux, heiress to the Deveraux lineage. This union represents a historic alliance between two of the most powerful supernatural families in existence..."

I pause, the weight of what I'm writing settling heavily on my shoulders. This isn't just an announcement—it's the death of my dreams, the final nail in the coffin of any hopes for a love-filled future.

But what choice do I have? The Ursa Clan needs this alliance. We've been isolated for too long, relying on our strength alone to maintain our position in the supernatural world. Times are changing. The old ways are dying, and if we don't adapt now, we'll be left behind.

And Cassandra... I close my eyes, remembering the fire in her gaze, the defiance in her stance. She's everything a queen should be—strong, intelligent, and fiercely loyal to her family. In another life, perhaps we could have been happy together. But her heart belongs to another, and mine...

My eyes drift back to Luciana's photograph. Mine will *always* belong to her.

The rain outside intensifies, drumming against the windows with renewed vigor. Magic stirs within me, an involuntary surge of power responding to the havoc in my heart. The storm is my creation, I realize. Dark clouds roil overhead, mirroring the gloom that has settled over my soul. Lightning flashes, a brief spark of anger illuminating the Parisian skyline. And the thunder that follows, rumbles as a low growl that could easily be mistaken for my bear's mournful cry.

I set down my pen, running a hand through my hair in frustration. This weather magic, unbidden and raw, is a stark reminder of the power I wield—and the responsibility that comes with it. Even in my darkest moments, my magic seeks an outlet, shaping the world around me. It's both a blessing and a curse, this ability to affect my environment so profoundly.

I take a deep breath, trying to center myself, to rein in the storm both outside and within. But the rain continues to fall, a relentless downpour that shows no signs of abating. Like my duty, like my grief, it stretches on with no end in sight.

With a heavy sigh, I rise from my desk, pacing the length of the study. The shelves lining the walls are filled with ancient tomes, grimoires, and artifacts collected over centuries. Each one represents the legacy I'm sworn to protect, the history I'm bound to continue.

My fingers trail along the spines of the books, feeling the pulse of magic contained within. This is my heritage, my birthright. And yet, at this moment, it feels more like a prison than a privilege.

I stop at the window, looking out over the rain-soaked streets of Paris. The City of Light seems dim tonight. Somewhere out there, Cassandra is probably cursing my name, plotting ways to escape this arrangement. And who could blame her?

Gods! How did it come to this? When did my life become a series of obligations, each one taking me further from what I truly want? Oh, but what does it matter? What my heart truly desires lies now beyond my reach.

My reflection stares back at me in the rain-streaked glass, a ghostly apparition of the man I once was. For a moment, I see not myself, but Luciana standing beside me, her warm smile a balm to my weary soul. I blink, and she's gone—a cruel trick of the light and my own longing.

I press my forehead against the cool pane, closing my eyes. The patter of rain fades away, replaced by the echo of laughter and the bustle of a warm Roman evening. Against my will, I find myself falling into memories of a time when life was simpler, when *love* was all that mattered...

1

WHERE HOME IS

ome's cobblestone streets stretch out before me, bathed in the golden light of a setting sun. The air is warm, filled with the scent of blooming flowers and the promise of adventure. The aroma of freshly baked bread wafts from a nearby bakery, mingling with the rich scent of espresso from a bustling café. In the distance, the melodic strains of a street violinist play a familiar Italian tune, the music seeming to dance on the warm breeze. And there, walking beside me, her delicate hand clasped in mine, is Luciana.

"Gavriil," she says, her voice carrying the lilt of suppressed laughter, "are you sure you know where we're going?"

I turn to her, drinking in the sight of her flushed

cheeks and sparkling eyes. "Of course I do," I reply with mock indignation. "I am the Ursa King. I *always* know exactly where I am."

She raises an eyebrow, unconvinced. "Uh-huh. And that's why we've passed that same fountain three times now?"

I open my mouth to protest, but she's right. In my distraction—my overwhelming joy at simply being with her—I've led us in circles. Instead of admitting defeat, I pull her close, wrapping my arms around her waist.

"Perhaps," I murmur, my lips inches from hers, "I simply wanted to extend our walk. To keep you all to myself for a little longer."

Luciana's laugh, warm and rich, fills the air between us. "Oh, you smooth talker," she teases, but there's no hiding the affection in her eyes. "Fine, keep your secrets. But if we're late for dinner, *you're* the one explaining it to Natalya."

I lean in, capturing her lips in a soft kiss. The world around us fades away, and for a moment, I forget about everything else—the responsibilities waiting for me back in Saint Petersburg, the recent vampire attacks, the weight of the crown I bear. Here, with Luciana, I'm just a man in love.

When we part, I rest my forehead against hers,

savoring the closeness. "I suppose we should get going," I sigh, reluctantly loosening my hold on her waist. "Natalya will have my hide if we're late."

Luciana smiles, linking her arm through mine as we resume our walk. "She wouldn't dare. You're the big, bad Ursa King, remember?"

I chuckle, shaking my head. "You'd be surprised. Natalya's not one to be intimidated by titles. Besides, she's family. That trumps any royal status."

As we navigate the winding streets of Rome, our footsteps echo off the ancient cobblestones, smooth and worn from centuries of use. The rough texture of sun-warmed stone walls brushes against our arms as we stroll through narrow alleys, occasionally stepping into patches of cool shade.

I can't help but marvel at how different everything feels with Luciana by my side. The eternal city has always held a special place in my heart—a refuge from the pressures of leadership, a place where I can shed the mantle of Ursa King and just be Gavriil. But now, with her, it's transformed into something magical.

We turn a corner, and I finally spot the familiar facade of Natalya's new place. It's a charming little townhouse, nestled between two larger buildings.

Warm light spills from the windows, and the scent of something delicious wafts through the air.

"See?" I say, gesturing grandly. "I told you I knew where we were going."

Luciana rolls her eyes, but her smile is fond. "My hero," she teases, reaching up to pat my cheek. "However would I have found my way without you?"

Before I can retort, the front door swings open, revealing Natalya. My cousin's face lights up when she sees us, her arms already opening for a hug.

"There you are!" she exclaims, pulling first me, then Luciana into a warm embrace. "I was beginning to worry you'd gotten lost."

I shoot Luciana a pleading look, silently begging her not to reveal our earlier wanderings. She winks at me before turning to Natalya with an innocent smile.

"Oh, you know Gavriil," she says lightly, a mischievous glint in her eye. "He insisted on showing me around my own city. Apparently, the Ursa King knows Rome better than a local girl who's lived here her whole life."

Natalya laughs, shooting me an amused look. "Is that so? And how did that work out for you, cousin?"

I clear my throat, trying to maintain my dignity. "It was... an *educational* experience for all involved."

Luciana grins, linking her arm through mine.

"Oh yes, *very* educational. I learned that even mighty shifter kings can get turned around in Roman alleyways."

"Traitor," I mutter under my breath, but a smile tugs at my lips.

Natalya's eyes dance with mirth as she ushers us inside. "Well, I'm just glad you both made it. Come in, come in! Everyone else is already here."

As we step into the warmth of Natalya's home, Luciana leans in close, whispering, "Don't worry, your secret's safe with me... *mostly*."

I shake my head, chuckling softly. This woman will be the death of my reputation; but honestly, I couldn't care less. Her teasing is a balm to my soul, lightening the weight I carry even if just for a moment.

The sound of laughter and conversation drifts from the living room, and as we round the corner, I'm greeted by the sight of my family sprawled across various pieces of vintage furniture. Vlad is lounging in an armchair, a glass of wine dangling from his fingers as he regales Dima with some outrageous story. Dima's sister, Mila, is perched on the arm of the sofa, her head thrown back in laughter at whatever Vlad's saying. And there, curled up next to Mila, is my sister Samara, her eyes bright with amusement.

"Look who finally decided to grace us with their presence," Vlad calls out, raising his glass in our direction. "Did you get lost in your own city, Luciana?"

Luciana grins, stepping into the room with the ease of someone who's truly part of the family. "Not me," she says, jerking a thumb in my direction. "Your illustrious leader, on the other hand..."

A chorus of laughter erupts, and I feel my cheeks heat. "I was merely taking the scenic route," I protest weakly.

Dima snorts, raising an eyebrow. "Is *that* what we're calling it now? Because last I checked, getting lost isn't exactly a kingly trait."

"Oh, leave him alone," Mila says, though her eyes are twinkling with mischief. "I'm sure His Majesty had his reasons for the... *extended tour.*"

Samara leans forward, a sly smile on her face. "I'm quite sure. Though I suspect those reasons had less to do with sightseeing and more to do with a certain lovely tour guide."

I open my mouth to defend myself, but Luciana beats me to it. "Guilty as charged," she says, pressing a quick kiss to my cheek. "Though I have to say, for a man who can track a vampire across three countries, his sense of direction in a city is surprisingly poor."

Another round of laughter fills the room, and I

find myself joining in. It's moments like these—surrounded by family and close friends, free from the burdens of leadership—that I cherish most.

Natalya claps her hands, drawing everyone's attention. "Alright, alright. As much as I'm enjoying watching our mighty king squirm, dinner's ready. Everyone to the dining room!"

There's a flurry of movement as we all make our way across the hall. The large table is laden with dishes, the scent of rosemary and garlic filling the air. As we take our seats, I'm struck by how seamlessly Luciana fits into this group. She laughs at Vlad's jokes, engages in spirited debate with Dima about the merits of various fighting styles, and even whispers conspiratorially with Mila and Samara.

"So, Gavriil," Vlad says as we start passing dishes around, "now that you've thoroughly explored Rome's alleyways, any plans for the rest of your stay?"

I swallow a bite of roasted lamb before answering. "Well, I thought I might actually let Luciana show me around properly this time. Maybe see some sights that aren't the same fountain three times over."

Luciana nudges me with her elbow, grinning. "Oh, I don't know. I think that fountain grew quite fond of us. We might hurt its feelings if we don't visit again."

"Speaking of feelings," Samara chimes in, leaning across the table with a gleam in her eye, "when are you two lovebirds going to make things official? The clan's been buzzing with speculation."

I nearly choke on my wine, caught off guard by the sudden change in topic. Luciana, gods bless her, takes it in stride.

"You know how it is," she says airily, waving a hand. "We're taking things slow. After all, I have to make sure he can find his way back to my place before I commit to anything long-term."

The table erupts in laughter once more, and I feel a rush of affection for this incredible woman beside me. She handles my family—and the weight of my position—with such grace and humor.

"In all seriousness," Vlad says once the laughter dies down, "it's wonderful to see you both so happy. You deserve it, brother."

His words, sincere and heartfelt, touch something deep within me. I reach for Luciana's hand under the table, giving it a gentle squeeze. "Thank you," I say softly. "I count myself incredibly lucky."

The conversation flows easily after that, touching on everything from clan politics to Natalya's latest magical experiments. As the meal winds down and we move back to the living room with fresh glasses of wine, the atmosphere is light and jovial. That is, until a sharp knock at the door cuts through the laughter like a knife.

The room falls silent, all eyes turning towards the entrance. Natalya frowns, clearly not expecting any more guests. "I'll get it," she says, setting down her wine glass and moving towards the door.

Tension builds up in the air, my shifter instincts on high alert. Luciana must sense it too, because her hand finds mine, squeezing gently.

The door opens, and a familiar voice carries into the room. "Natalya, I... I'm sorry to intrude, but—"

Sasha's words cut off as he steps into view, his ice-blue eyes scanning the room before landing on me. The sight of my Enforcer, his pale blonde hair disheveled and his usually immaculate clothes rumpled from travel, sends a chill down my spine.

"Sasha," I say, rising to my feet. "What's wrong?"

The room is so quiet you could hear a pin drop. Natalya stands frozen in the doorway, her face a mask of conflicting emotions as she stares at her ex-boyfriend.

Sasha's gaze flicks briefly to Natalya before returning to me. "Your Majesty," he says, his voice tight with urgency. "I apologize for the interruption, but we have a situation. There have been... disturbances in Eastern Europe. Significant ones."

Vlad and Dima are on their feet now too, their expressions grim.

"What kind of disturbances?" Vlad asks, his earlier levity completely gone.

Sasha hesitates, his eyes darting around the room. "It's not something I can discuss openly," he says guardedly. Even after all we've been through, he's still uncertain of my brother's loyalty.

The weight of his words settles over the room like a heavy blanket. Luciana's hand tightens in mine, and when I look at her, I see worry etched across her features.

"You may speak openly," I answer with a nod, lifting any hesitation lingering in the room.

"It's those pesky rival clans," my Enforcer finally says, his brow furrowed.

"Their attacks are becoming more frequent," Dima intervenes, "more organized. It's almost as if they're testing our defenses."

I nod, feeling the weight of leadership settling back onto my shoulders. "We'll need to increase patrols along the borders, maybe reach out to some of our allies for additional support." A pause to brace myself. "How bad is it?" I ask Sasha, dreading the answer.

My Enforcer's face is grim. "Bad enough that I came personally instead of sending a message… We need to move, Your Majesty. Tonight, if possible."

I close my eyes for a moment. The carefree evening with family and loved ones suddenly feels like a distant memory.

"Alright," I say, opening my eyes and straightening my spine. "Vlad, Dima, you're with me. Sasha, make the necessary arrangements for our departure."

As the room bursts into activity, I turn to Luciana, my heart heavy. "I'm sorry about this, my love," I murmur, bringing her hand to my lips.

Vlad leans forward, his eyes intense. "Brother, I've got some contacts who might be able to provide insight. Let me make a few calls before you leave… It's not much, but it's a start."

"I appreciate it," I reply, and I mean each word.

Sasha pulls a chair close, Dima joins in, and as we delve deeper into strategy and planning, I notice Luciana slip away towards the kitchen before disappearing around the corner.

A few minutes later, I excuse myself from the conversation, following the path Luciana took. I find her in the pantry, reaching for a bottle on a high shelf.

"Need a hand?" I ask, stepping close behind her.

She turns, a smile playing at the corners of her mouth. "I don't know. Can you reach it without getting lost?"

I chuckle, easily plucking the bottle from the shelf. "I think I can manage," I purr, gliding a hand around her waist, instinctively pulling her towards me. "Though I must say… I'm quite enjoying this particular detour."

Luciana's eyes darken slightly as she looks up at me. "Is that so?"

In answer, I set the bottle aside and pull her closer, capturing her lips in a deep kiss. She responds immediately, her arms winding around my neck as she presses herself against me. The world narrows down to just this—the softness of her lips, the warmth of her body, the quiet sounds of pleasure she makes as I deepen the kiss.

When we finally part, both breathing heavily, Luciana's smile comes tinged with a hint of sorrow. Finally, she says, "If this is your way of making up for getting us lost earlier, I might have to let you lead more often."

I laugh softly, pressing my forehead against hers. "Noted. Though, I much prefer *this kind* of exploration."

She responds with light amusement, but I glimpse the sadness brewing in her glimmering eyes, sense the turmoil shadowing her heart. So far, I've failed to reveal to her my nature as an empath—figured coming out as a bear shifter and warlock was enough of a shock already.

"Hey," I breathe soothingly, my hand gently cupping the side of her face. "What's wrong, love? You can tell me."

Luciana's eyes meet mine, a storm of emotions swirling within them. She takes a shaky breath, her fingers curling into the fabric of my shirt.

"I... I don't want you to go," she whispers, her voice barely audible. "I know you have to, I understand that. But I can't shake this feeling of dread."

I pull her to me, wrapping my arms tightly around her. "Talk to me, please. What are you afraid of?"

She buries her face in my chest, the warmth of her tears seeping through my shirt. "I'm afraid of losing you," she confesses, her words muffled against me. "We've only just found each other, Gavriil. What we have... it's everything I've ever wanted, everything I never knew I needed. And now you're leaving, rushing into danger, and I..."

Her voice breaks, and I feel my heart constrict. I

gently lift her chin, meeting her tear-filled gaze. "Luciana, my love," I say softly, "I promise you, I *will* come back. Nothing in this world could keep me from returning to you."

She shakes her head, a sad smile on her lips. "You can't promise that, Gavriil. You're the Ursa King. Your life is full of dangers I can barely comprehend. What if... what if this is the last time I see you?"

The raw fear in her voice strikes me to my core. I cup her face in my hands, pressing my forehead to hers. "Listen to me," I say, my voice low and intense. "You are my heart, Luciana. My soul. Wherever I go, whatever battles I face, I carry you with me. And that love, that connection, will *always* bring me back to you."

She closes her eyes, leaning into my touch. "I want to believe that," she whispers. "I do. But I'm just a human, Gavriil. I can't fight alongside you, can't protect you. I feel so... helpless."

I brush my thumbs across her cheeks, wiping away her tears. "You protect me in ways you don't even realize," I tell her. "Your love gives me strength, gives me a reason to fight harder, to be better. You make me want to create a world where we can be together without fear."

Luciana opens her eyes, and I see a glimmer of hope amidst the worry. "Promise me something?" she asks.

"Anything," I respond without hesitation.

"Promise me you'll be careful," she begins. "That you won't take unnecessary risks. And... promise me you'll come back to me as soon as you can."

I lean in, brushing my lips against hers in a tender kiss. "I promise," I murmur against her mouth. "I will be as careful as I can be, and I will move heaven and earth to return to you quickly."

She nods, taking a deep breath as if to steady herself. "*Bene*," she says, her voice stronger now. "*Va bene*. I... I understand you have to go. Just... don't forget about me while you're out there being all heroic and kingly."

I find myself chuckling, relieved to see a hint of her usual humor returning. "Forget about you? Impossible. You, my love, are utterly unforgettable."

Luciana manages a small smile, though I can still see the worry lingering in her eyes. "I love you, Gavriil," she says softly. "More than I ever thought possible."

"And I love you," I reply, pouring every ounce of emotion I can into those words. "You are my heart, my home… No matter where I go, I'll always find my way back to you."

We stay like that for a moment longer, holding each other in the quiet of the pantry. And as we reluctantly break apart, I look at her beautiful face, memorizing every detail. I know it might be the last time I see her for a while, or even… I push the thought aside, refusing to entertain such morbid musings. Instead, I focus on the here and now, the feel of her warmth still lingering on my skin.

Her intoxicating scent envelops me, a heady mixture of jasmine and something uniquely Luciana. The bear within me stirs, awakened by her nearness. My body responds instantly, desire coursing through my veins like liquid fire. I inch closer, unable to resist the magnetic pull between us.

"Luciana," I growl, my lips brushing the graceful slope of her neck. "I want you."

Luciana gasps, her body trembling under my touch. "Gavriil… we shouldn't… Not here, not now…" she protests weakly, her voice laced with desire.

"I know, baby," I growl against her ear, inhaling her intoxicating scent. "But I can't help myself. I want you too much." My hands slide down her waist to caress her thighs, leaving goosebumps in their wake.

Her resolve finally crumbles like sandcastles

before the tide. "Yes," she moans, arching her back and inviting me closer. "I need you."

In response, I lift her up onto the nearby countertop, planting her legs on either side of my hips. The dim light casts flickering shadows on her flushed skin as I slowly push up her skirt.

As much as I'd like to savor every inch of her delicious skin, time is running short. We both know it without saying a word. With shaking hands, I unfasten my trousers, releasing my aching arousal. A brief gasp escapes her, and Luciana's eyes darken with lust as she takes in the sight of me—hard and wanting for only her.

"Shh… Don't make a sound," I growl, my voice edged with control.

"Gavriil," she whimpers again, rocking her hips against mine in a silent plea for more contact between us.

Giving in to our primal lust, I position myself at her entrance, my hasty breaths hot on her neck as I pause for a fleeting second. "I've wanted you all day long," I grunt out, then plunge into her wet heat. Her walls tighten around me, and a shudder courses through her body as she arches her back, burying me even deeper inside her.

Harder and faster, we move, our passionate

rhythm echoing off the pantry walls. My hands grip her hips as hers dig into the countertop, nails embedded in the wood. Our moans fill the room, intermingling with the flickering light and the heady scent of spices.

Luciana's eyes lock onto mine, and in them, I see the same raging inferno that burns within me—a fire that has smoldered between us for months. "Yes," she pants out, urging me onward, her body trembling beneath mine.

Lost in the moment, I pick up speed, angling my hips to hit that one spot that always sends her over the edge. Her muscles clench around me, and she bites her lower lip to muffle a moan.

"Gavriil!" she gasps. When she crumbles, about to release a cry of pleasure, I silence her with a feverish kiss. It's all the encouragement I need as I thrust deep one last time before my own climax overtakes me, our release crashing over us like a tidal wave.

As our breathing slows and the world rights itself once more, I gently lower her onto shaky legs. We stand there panting in each other's arms, pressed against the cool pantry wall. And we stay like that for a moment, just holding each other in the quiet of the room. It's a stolen moment of peace, a brief respite from the responsibilities waiting for us outside.

"I love you, Luciana," I whisper into her hair, my heart finally settling into a steady rhythm. "Gods, I love you."

She gasps, still catching her breath from the exertion.

"We should probably head back," I utter, though I make no move to release her.

"We probably should," she whispers, burying her face in my chest. "Before they send a search party."

My hold tightens a bit more as I sigh dramatically. "I suppose you're right. After all, I have a reputation as a poor navigator to uphold now."

Luciana laughs, and the sound is music to my ears.

A moment later, we make our way back to the living room, hands clasped and slightly rumpled. We're instantly met with knowing looks and barely suppressed smiles.

"Ah, there you are," Vlad says, his voice dripping with mischief. "Got lost on the way to the kitchen, did you?"

I open my mouth to retort, but Luciana speaks first. "Actually, Gavriil was just giving me a tour of Natalya's pantry. Did you know he's an expert on the organizational systems of kitchen storage?"

The room dissolves into laughter once more, and

as I take my seat, pulling Luciana down beside me. I'm struck by how right this feels. The teasing, the laughter, the love—it's everything I never knew I needed.

As the night wears on and the conversation flows, joy swells in my heart—despite the weight of the constant threats and the recent vampire attacks, the losses we've suffered. It all becomes lighter, more manageable, if only for a little while.

When the night is spent, and we're saying our goodbyes, Natalya pulls me aside. "It's so good to see you like this, cousin," she says softly. "Happy, at ease with your role as our king... Luciana's good for you."

I glance over at Luciana, engrossed in conversation with Mila and Samara. "She is," I agree. "More than I think she realizes."

Natalya squeezes my arm. "Don't ever let her go, Gavriil. Some things are worth fighting for, no matter the cost."

Her words stay with me as Luciana and I make our way to the line of Ursa vehicles parked along the street. The night is cool now, the earlier warmth having faded with the setting sun. Luciana shivers slightly, and I wrap an arm around her, pulling her close.

My gaze cuts to Sasha, lounging in a sleek Maybach while Dima stands guard next to our SUV, ready to take Luciana home.

I lean in close to her, my voice dripping with longing as I whisper, "I'll miss you. Terribly. Constantly. Painfully..."

But just when I think she'll melt in my arms, she stops me with a determined glint in her eye and says, "Then don't leave without me."

My heart skips a beat at the thought of her joining us on our dangerous mission. For a moment, I'm speechless. The thought of Luciana in the midst of the danger we're heading into sends a chill down my spine. "Luciana, I can't ask you to—"

But before I can protest, she cuts me off. "You're not asking, Gavriil. I'm *telling*. We face this life together now, no matter what the risks may be."

Torn between admiration for her fierce spirit and concern for her safety, I shake my head and try to reason with her. "It's too dangerous. I couldn't bear it if something happened to you."

Luciana's eyes soften, but her resolve doesn't waver. "And I couldn't bear sitting here, not knowing if you're safe. At least if I'm with you, I can watch your back."

"You don't know what you're getting into," I argue weakly, even as I feel my resistance crumbling.

She cups my face in her hands, her gaze steady and sure. "Maybe not. But I know what I'm leaving behind if I stay. A life half-lived, always wondering, always worrying... That's not the kind of life I want, Gavriil. I want to be by your side, through everything."

I close my eyes, leaning into her touch. The thought of having her with me, of not having to say goodbye, is intoxicating. But the risks...

"Gavriil," she says softly, drawing my attention back to her. "You told me I was your heart, your home. Well, you're mine too. Home isn't a place for me anymore. It's wherever you are."

Her words break through the last of my resistance. I pull her close, pressing my forehead to hers. "You're sure about this?" I ask, giving her one last chance to change her mind.

Luciana nods, a smile playing on her lips. "I've never been more sure of anything in my life."

I take a deep breath, then nod. "Alright," I say, trepidation and excitement tangling in my core. "We do this together."

Her face lights up with joy, and she throws her

arms around my neck. I lift her off her feet, spinning her around once before setting her down.

I set her down gently, but I can't bear to let her go just yet. My hand glides along her soft jawline, tracing the curve I've come to know so well. Her skin is warm beneath my touch, alive with the joy that radiates from her very being. Our eyes lock, and in that moment, I'm lost in the depths of her gaze. The world around us fades away, leaving only Luciana and the overwhelming love I feel for her. My thumb brushes her cheek, and I'm struck once again by how perfectly she fits in my arms, how right it feels to hold her close.

"My fate hangs from your every breath, your every move… I love you, body and soul, my love. You must know that," I murmur against the soft strands of her hair.

"And I love you," she replies without hesitation, her voice overflowing with warmth and certainty.

Hand in hand, we stride towards the waiting car, our hearts beating as one. The sense of rightness that washes over me is undeniable.

Sasha raises an eyebrow as we approach, undoubtedly taking note of Luciana's presence. I give him a small nod and he opens the car door without a word.

We glide into the backseat, Luciana's hand tightly

clasped in mine. The car pulls away from the curb, carrying us towards an uncertain future. But as I gaze at my beloved mate, her eyes gleaming with love and determination, I know that no matter what trials we encounter, we will face them united. And that realization, above all else, grants me the courage to move forward.

2

THROWING AXES

The harsh wind howls outside, carrying flurries of snow that dance past the frost-covered windows of my study. I stand before the hearth, allowing the warmth of the crackling fire to seep into my bones. It's been a month since we returned to Saint Petersburg, our territory now secure and the immediate threats quelled. Our borders are under constant watch, a network of loyal packs keeping vigilant guard. This respite has allowed us to finally breathe, to settle into some semblance of normalcy.

Yet even as I revel in this hard-won peace, I'm still amazed by how the novelty of the Russian winter has yet to wear off for Luciana. Despite the bone-chilling cold that would send most humans scurrying for warmer climes, she embraces each snowfall with childlike wonder. Her enthusiasm for this harsh beauty reminds me daily of the joy she's brought into my life, a warmth that rivals even the fiercest hearth fire.

As if summoned by my thoughts, the door creaks open, and she enters, cheeks flushed from the cold, snowflakes still clinging to her golden hair. My breath catches in my throat at the sight of her. Even bundled up in layers of wool and fur, she's the most beautiful thing I've ever seen.

"There you are," Luciana says, a smile lighting up her face. "I was beginning to think you'd gotten lost in your own home."

I chuckle, moving to meet her. "I'll have you know, I'm much better at navigating my ancestral estate than the streets of Rome."

She raises an eyebrow, her eyes twinkling with mischief. "Is that so? Because I distinctly remember having to rescue you from the east wing yesterday."

"I was merely... inspecting the lesser-used corridors," I defend weakly, pulling her into my arms.

Luciana laughs, the sound warming me more thoroughly than any fire ever could. "Of course you were, Your Majesty. How silly of me to think otherwise."

I lean down, pressing a soft kiss to her lips. "What brings you to my lair, my love? Not that I'm complaining, mind you."

She pulls back slightly, excitement dancing in her eyes. "Well, I was thinking... You promised to teach me how to throw axes, remember? And it's such a beautiful day outside..."

I glance out the window at the swirling snow. "*Beautiful*, she says," I mutter, shaking my head in fond exasperation. "You do realize it's freezing out there, right?"

Luciana rolls her eyes. "Oh, come on. Where's your sense of adventure? Besides, I thought bears loved the cold."

"We do," I admit. "But you, my dear, are decidedly *not* a bear."

She pouts, and I feel my resolve crumbling. "Please, Gavriil? I've been cooped up inside for days. I need to do something before I go stir-crazy."

I sigh, knowing I'm fighting a losing battle. "Alright, alright... Let me grab my coat, and we'll head out to the training grounds."

Luciana's face lights up with joy, and she bounces on her toes in excitement. "God, yes! Thank you, thank you, thank you!"

It's impossible for me not to laugh at her enthusiasm. "You're entirely too excited about the prospect of hurling sharp objects through the air."

She grins, unrepentant. "What can I say? I like living dangerously. After all, I did fall in love with the Ursa King."

My heart swells at her words. Even after all this time, I find it hard to believe that this incredible woman chose me, chose this life with all its complications and dangers.

We make our way through the winding corridors of my estate, Luciana's hand warm in mine. As we pass by windows, I catch glimpses of the snow-covered grounds, the bare trees standing like sentinels against the white landscape.

Finally, we reach the heavy wooden doors that lead to the courtyard. I pause, turning to Luciana. "Are you sure about this? We could always practice indoors, you know."

She shakes her head, determination etched on her face. "Nope. If I'm going to learn, I want to do it properly. Outside, in the elements, just like a real warrior."

I can't resist the urge to smile when I hear her words. "As you wish, my fierce little human."

We step out into the biting cold, and I hear Luciana's sharp intake of breath. The snow crunches beneath our feet as we make our way to the training grounds. The axe-throwing range is a simple setup—a series of wooden targets set at varying distances, with a rack of axes nearby.

I lead Luciana to the rack, selecting a lighter axe that should suit her frame. "Now," I begin, slipping into what she calls my 'teacher voice', "the key to throwing an axe is all in the stance and the release."

I demonstrate, my body easing through the familiar motions. The weight of the axe feels comforting in my hand, the wooden handle smooth and cool against my palm. As I release it, there's a moment of whistling air before the satisfying thunk of metal embedding into wood reaches my ears.

Luciana's eyes are wide with admiration. "Wow," she breathes. "That was... incredibly hot."

I feel a surge of pride at her words. "Your turn," I say, handing her the axe.

She takes it, testing its weight in her hand. "Okay, here goes nothing."

I move behind her, adjusting her stance with gentle touches. "Feet shoulder-width apart," I murmur, my hands on her hips. "Dominant foot slightly back. Now, bring the axe up..."

Luciana follows my instructions, her body tense with concentration. "Like this?"

"Perfect," I purr into her ear, my voice low. "Now, when you throw, it's all in the wrist. Let the axe do the work."

She nods, takes a deep breath, and throws. The axe spins through the air... and lands with a dull thud in the snow, several feet short of the target.

Luciana's shoulders slump in disappointment. "Well, *that* was embarrassing."

I chuckle, pressing a kiss to her temple. "Nobody's perfect on their first try, love. It takes practice."

She straightens, a determined glint in her eye. "Again," she says, reaching for another axe.

We spend the next hour practicing, Luciana's throws gradually improving. She may not have the natural strength of a shifter, but what she lacks in power, she makes up for in sheer determination. By the time the sun begins to set, painting the snowy landscape in hues of pink and gold, she's managed to hit the target more often than not.

"I did it!" she cries as her latest throw sticks in the outer ring of the target. She turns to me, face flushed with exertion and joy, snowflakes clinging to her eyelashes.

I can't resist, and pull her into my arms, spinning her around as she laughs. "You're a natural," I say, setting her down but keeping her close.

Luciana grins up at me, her eyes sparkling. "I had a good teacher."

"Is that so?" I purr, leaning in close. "And what *other* skills would you like me to teach you, my love?"

Her breath hitches, and I feel her heart rate quicken. "I'm sure you could think of a few things," she says, her voice low and teasing.

I'm about to close the distance between us when a snowball hits me squarely in the back of the head. I whirl around to see Samara standing a few yards away, another snowball already formed in her hand.

"If you two are quite finished with your little love fest," she calls out, amusement clear in her voice, "some of us would like to use the training grounds for actual training."

Luciana laughs, the sound bright in the crisp air. "You're just jealous because you can't hit a target as well as I can," she teases.

Sam's eyebrows shoot up. "Is that a challenge, *little human*?" she taunts back.

I groan, already seeing where this is going. "Luciana, love, maybe we should—"

But she's already striding towards the axe rack, a competitive fire in her eyes. "You're on, witchy girl. Let's see what you've got."

What follows is possibly the most ridiculous axe-throwing competition I've ever witnessed. Sam, of course, has years of experience on her side. But Luciana's determination and beginner's luck keep her in the game. They trade playful insults and boasts, their laughter echoing across the snowy grounds.

I stand back, watching with amusement and pride. Seeing Luciana like this—confident, playful, fully embracing this new world she's entered—fills me with a warmth that has nothing to do with the exertion of throwing axes.

As the light fades and the temperature drops further, I finally call an end to their competition. "Alright, you two. As much as I'm enjoying watching you make fools of yourselves, it's getting late. And some of us," I add, looking pointedly at each of them, "don't have the luxury of fur coats to keep us warm."

Luciana pouts but doesn't argue. She's shivering slightly, though I'm sure she'd deny it if asked. "Fine, fine. But this isn't over," she tells Sam, pointing a finger at her in mock threat.

Sam grins, bumping Luciana's shoulder affectionately. "Wouldn't dream of it, sweet sister. We'll have a rematch soon."

As we make our way back to the house, Luciana tucked securely under my arm, I'm struck by how she's become an integral part of my world. She banters with Sam as if they've known each other for years, has charmed even the most stoic members of my clan, and faces every new challenge with a determination that never fails to impress me.

"What are you thinking about?" Luciana asks, tilting her head to look up at me.

I smile down at her, pressing a kiss to her cold-reddened nose. "Just how lucky I am to have you here with me."

She beams, snuggling closer. "There's nowhere else I'd rather be."

As we enter the warmth of the house, shaking off snow and removing layers of winter gear, I'm struck by a sudden, overwhelming wave of love for this woman. She's given up so much to be here with me—her home, her business, the life she knew. And yet, she faces each day with a smile and an enthusiasm that can only lift my spirits.

"Come on," I say, taking her hand. "Let's get you warmed up."

We make our way to our chambers, where a fire is already crackling merrily in the hearth. Luciana sighs in contentment as the warmth envelops us, her shivering gradually subsiding.

"I think I'm starting to understand why bears

hibernate," she says, moving closer to the fire and holding out her hands to warm them.

I chuckle, coming up behind her and wrapping my arms around her waist. "Feeling a bit chilly, are we?"

She leans back against me, her sensuous body fitting perfectly against mine. "Maybe a little," she confesses. "But it was worth it. I had fun today."

"I'm glad," I murmur, nuzzling into her hair. "Though I have to say, watching you throw axes was... quite stimulating."

Luciana turns in my arms, a mischievous glint in her eye. "Really? And here I thought you were just impressed by my natural talent."

I growl low in my throat, pulling her closer. "Oh, I was definitely impressed. But mostly, I was thinking about how sexy you looked, all flushed and determined."

Her breath hitches, and I feel her heart rate quicken. "Is that so?" she says, her voice low and teasing. "And what do you plan to do about it, Your Majesty?"

In answer, I capture her lips in a searing kiss. She responds immediately, her arms winding around my neck as she presses herself against me. I lift her easily, carrying her to the bed without breaking the kiss.

As I lay her down, I take a moment to just look at her. Her wavy hair is spread out on the pillow like a golden halo, her cheeks flushed with desire, her eyes dark with want. "You are so beautiful," I breathe, almost reverently.

Luciana smiles up at me, reaching out to cup my face. "And you, my love, are wearing far too many clothes."

I laugh, the sound rumbling deep in my chest. "As my lady commands," I say, making quick work of my shirt.

A tangle of limbs and sheets follows, of whispered endearments and passionate cries. We come together with a familiarity born of countless nights like this, yet each time feels new, exciting, as if we're discovering each other all over again.

After, as we lay tangled together, Luciana's head resting on my chest, I find myself marveling once again at the turn my life has taken. A year ago, I was alone, weighed down by the responsibilities of leadership and the losses I'd suffered. And now...

Luciana's fingers dance across my skin, tracing intricate patterns that send shivers down my spine. She shifts, propping herself up on an elbow to gaze down at me, her eyes filled with curiosity and warmth.

"Your mind seems far away," she murmurs, her voice soft and inviting. "Care to share the journey?"

I draw her close, my lips meeting hers in a kiss as soft as a whisper. When we part, our faces still mere inches apart, I'm overwhelmed by the depth of my feelings for her.

"Sometimes," I breathe, my words a caress against her skin, "I wonder what twist of fate brought you into my life. Whatever cosmic alignment, whatever divine intervention led me to you... I'm grateful for it with every beat of my heart."

A soft laugh bubbles from Luciana's lips, her eyes twinkling with amusement and affection. "My fierce Ursa King," she murmurs, nestling back against my chest, "who knew you had such a silver tongue?"

Her warmth seeps into me, chasing away the last vestiges of the day's worries. Slowly, a profound sense of peace washes over me, as steady and sure as the rise and fall of Luciana's breath. In this quiet interlude between wakefulness and dreams, I'm struck by the realization that this—her presence, our love—is the eye of calm in the storm of my life as Ursa King.

3

SPELLS AND THREATS

The next morning dawns bright and clear, the world outside our window transformed into a glittering expanse of white. Sunlight streams through the frost-etched glass, casting intricate patterns across our bed. I've been awake for a while, content to watch Luciana sleep, her features softened in repose, a picture of serenity against the crisp white sheets.

As if sensing my gaze, Luciana stirs beside me. Her eyes flutter open, revealing those hazel depths I could lose myself in for eternity. She stretches languidly, her lithe body arching under the thick quilts that cover our bed.

"Доброе утро, красавица." *Good morning, beautiful*, I murmur, pressing a kiss to her forehead.

She smiles up at me, her expression still soft with sleep. "Mmm, good morning," she replies, her voice husky. "What time is it?"

I glance at the ornate clock on the mantle, an Alexeev family heirloom that's ticked away the hours for generations. "Just past nine," I answer, surprised. "We've slept in."

Luciana's eyes widen, sleep vanishing in an instant. "Nine? Oh no, I'm late for my lesson with Samara!"

A chuckle escapes me as she scrambles out of bed, the quilts falling away to reveal her silk nightgown. She rushes to the wardrobe, pulling out clothes with frantic energy.

"I'm sure she'll understand, love," I say, propping myself up on one elbow to watch her. "She knows how... distracting I can be for you."

She throws a playful glare over her shoulder, her cheeks flushing at the memory of last night's *distractions*. "Don't look so smug," she scolds, though I can see the smile tugging at her lips. "This is your fault, you know."

I hold up my hands in mock surrender, not even trying to hide my grin. "I take full responsibility. Shall I make it up to you with breakfast? I could have the kitchen prepare those blini you love so much."

Luciana pauses in the act of pulling on a sweater, temptation clear on her face. "That's not fair," she groans. "You know I can't resist your blini." She shakes her head, resolve firming. "But I really should go. Your sister has been so patient with me, trying to teach me basic protection spells. I don't want to disappoint her."

I sit up, watching her with pride and amusement. In the weeks she's been here, Luciana has thrown herself into learning everything she can about our world. From Samara's magic lessons to combat training with Sasha and Dima, she's determined to carve out a place for herself here.

"You could never disappoint her," I murmur. "Or any of us, for that matter. You've taken to this life so naturally, Luciana. It's like you were born into it."

She pauses in her rush, coming over to sit on the edge of the bed. "It's not always easy," she admits, taking my hand. "There's so much to learn, so many rules and traditions. Sometimes, I feel like I'm fumbling in the dark."

I squeeze her hand reassuringly. "You're doing amazingly well. And you know you can always come to me if you're feeling overwhelmed, right?"

Luciana nods. "I know. And I love you for it. But right now, I really do need to go, before Samara decides to come looking for me herself. You know how creative she can get with those location spells of hers."

I laugh softly, reluctantly releasing her hand. The loss of contact is immediate, a slight ache that reminds me of how deeply she's woven into my life. "Go on then, my love," I say, my voice warm with affection. "I'll see you at dinner? I promise to have a plate of steaming blini waiting, topped with that wild berry jam you adore."

Luciana's eyes light up at the prospect, a smile spreading across her face that rivals the morning sun. "It's a date," she says with a playful wink. She leans in, pressing a quick kiss to my cheek, her lips soft and warm against my skin. And then she's off, gone in a whirlwind of golden hair and floral perfume.

I flop back onto the pillows, a smile playing at my lips. Even after a month of living together, I'm still not entirely sure how I got so lucky. The thought of spending the rest of my life with Luciana by my side fills me with a joy I never thought possible.

But as always, duty calls. With a sigh, I drag myself out of bed and begin preparing for the day ahead. There are reports to review, meetings to attend, and the ever-present threat of enemy activity to monitor.

As I dress, my mind wanders to the upcoming full moon. It will be Luciana's first time witnessing a mass shift, and while she's excited, I can't help but worry. The bear within me is always closer to the surface during the full moon, more primal, more possessive. How will she react to seeing that side of me?

A knock at the door interrupts my musings. "Enter," I call out, fastening the last button on my shirt.

Sasha steps in, a stack of papers in his hand. "Good morning, Your Majesty. I have the latest reports from our border patrols."

"Walk with me," I command, striding past him into the hallway. The plush carpet muffles our footsteps as we move through the dimly lit corridor, portraits of my ancestors watching our passage with solemn eyes.

I nod, gesturing for him to continue as we descend the grand staircase. "Anything urgent?"

He hesitates, and I feel my stomach drop. "There have been... sightings. Near the eastern border."

"Vampires?" I ask, though I already know the answer.

"Rogue wolf shifters," Sasha replies grimly. "A small group, three or four at most. They've made no aggressive moves yet, but their presence alone is concerning."

We reach the bottom of the stairs, our path taking us through the cavernous main hall. The morning light streams through the tall windows, catching dust motes in its golden beams.

My jaw clenches, the muscles in my neck tensing as the implications of Sasha's report sink in. The brief respite of domestic bliss evaporates, replaced by the all-too-familiar weight of responsibility.

"What of our allies?" I ask, my voice low and controlled despite the surge of adrenaline coursing through me. "Have the neighboring packs been alerted to this... development?"

"Yes, Your Majesty. They've increased their patrols and are on high alert."

We arrive at my study, the heavy oak door swinging open silently at my touch. I stride to the window, looking out over the snow-covered grounds of the estate. In the distance, I can see Luciana making her way to the Winter Garden, where Samara practices her craft, her golden hair a bright spot against the white landscape. The sight of her, so small and vulnerable in this harsh world of ours, strengthens my resolve.

"Double the border patrols," I say, turning back to Sasha.

Sasha nods, making a note. "And what of the full moon gathering? Should we consider postponing?"

I shake my head. "No. We can't let fear dictate our actions. The gathering will proceed as planned. But increase security, just in case."

"Very well, Your Majesty. Is there anything else?"

I hesitate, my gaze drifting back to the window. Luciana has disappeared from view now, but I can still picture her, determined and brave, in the face of this new world she's entered.

"Yes," I say finally. "I want Luciana to start advanced combat training. Not just the basics she's been learning with you and Dima. I want her trained as if she were one of us."

Sasha's eyebrows rise in surprise. "Are you sure that's wise? She's only human, after all."

I fix him with a stern look. "She may be human, but she's also the future queen of our clan. She needs to be able to defend herself."

Understanding dawns in Sasha's eyes. "Of course. I'll make the arrangements immediately."

As he turns to leave, I call out, "And Sasha? Don't tell Luciana about the wolf sightings. Not yet. I don't want to worry her unnecessarily."

He nods, though I can see the doubt in his eyes. "As you wish, Your Majesty."

Once I'm alone again, I sink into the chair behind my desk, the weight of my decisions heavy on my mind. Am I doing the right thing, keeping this from Luciana? She's proven time and again that she's stronger than she looks, more capable than even she realizes. But the thought of her in danger, of those rogue monsters anywhere near her...

The bear within me growls, itching to be released, to hunt down any threat to my mate. I take a deep breath, pushing the urge down. Now is not the time for rash actions. We need strategy, planning.

I force myself to focus on the reports Sasha brought, losing myself in the details of clan business. But even as I work, a part of my mind remains fixed on Luciana, on the challenges that lie ahead.

Hours pass as I immerse myself in reports and strategy plans. The steady tick of the clock on my desk is the only sound breaking the silence of my study. Just as I'm about to reach for another document, a rapid knock at the door pulls me from my concentration.

Before I can respond, the door flies open, and Luciana bursts in, her face alight with excitement.

"Gavriil, you won't believe what happened!" she exclaims, her eyes sparkling as she rushes towards me. She holds out her hand, and I can see a faint shimmer of magic surrounding it. "I cast a protection spell! A *real* one!"

Pride swells in my chest, mingling with a sense of awe. "That's incredible, Luciana. I knew you had it in you."

She beams, her joy infectious. "Sam says it's not very strong yet, but it's definitely there. She has a theory, actually." Luciana's voice drops to a conspiratorial whisper. "She thinks that because my *nonna* was a *strega*, there might be more magic in my blood than we first thought. Sam wants to explore it further, see if we can awaken more of my potential."

I pull her close, pressing a kiss to her forehead. "I'm not surprised. You've always been extraordinary, my love. Magic or no magic." I pause, considering the implications. "But if Samara is right, this could change everything. How do you feel about it?"

Luciana's eyes meet mine, a mix of excitement and uncertainty swirling in their depths. "Honestly? I'm a little scared. But mostly, I'm thrilled. To be able to protect myself, to truly be a part of your world in every way… it's more than I ever dreamed possible."

She beams at me, then seems to notice the pile of papers on my desk for the first time. "Oh, I'm sorry. Am I interrupting important king business?"

I shake my head, reaching out to pull her into my lap. "Nothing that can't wait. Tell me more about your lesson."

As Luciana launches into a detailed description of her magic lesson, complete with dramatic reenactments that have me chuckling, I feel the last of my tension melting away. This is what matters, I realize. Not the reports or the politics or even the looming threat of rogue shifters. This moment, right here, with the woman I love in my arms, laughing and full of life.

"What is it?" Luciana asks, noticing my contemplative expression.

I smile, pressing a kiss to her temple. "I'm just thinking about how much I love you. And how proud I am of everything you've accomplished."

She blushes, ducking her head. "I still have so much to learn."

"We all do," I assure her. "But you're doing amazingly well. In fact…" I hesitate, wondering if now is the right time to bring this up.

Luciana tilts her head, curiosity shining in her eyes. "In fact, what?"

I take a deep breath. "I've asked Sasha to arrange for you to start advanced combat training."

Her eyes widen in surprise. "Advanced? But I've barely mastered the basics."

"You're selling yourself short," I tell her. "Sasha and Dima have both said you're a quick learner. And..." I trail off, not wanting to worry her with talk of increased danger.

But Luciana, perceptive as always, picks up on my hesitation. "And what, Gavriil? What aren't you telling me?"

I sigh, knowing I can't keep this from her. It wouldn't be fair, and besides, she deserves to know the truth. "There have been some... concerning reports from our border patrols. Nothing definite yet, but..."

"Vampires?" she asks, her voice barely above a whisper.

I tighten my arms around her. "Wolf shifters. We're increasing security measures, but I want you to be prepared. Just in case."

To my surprise, instead of fear, I see determination flash in Luciana's eyes. "Okay," she says, straightening her spine. "When do we start?"

I can't resist laughing at how eager she is. "Tomorrow, if you're up for it. But Luciana, this won't be easy. It'll be intense, grueling even."

She meets my gaze steadily. "I can handle it. I'm not some delicate flower, Gavriil. I'm your mate, the future queen of this clan. If there's danger coming, I want to be ready to face it."

My heart swells with pride and love. This incredible woman never ceases to amaze me. "That's my girl," I murmur, pulling her in for a kiss.

When we part, Luciana's eyes are shining with excitement and determination. "So, who's going to be training me? Sasha? Dima?"

I shake my head. "No. For this, I want the best. You'll be training with *me*."

Her eyebrows shoot up. "You? But I thought you were too busy with clan business."

"Nothing is more important than your safety," I tell her seriously. "Besides, who better to teach you than the Ursa King himself?"

Luciana grins, a mischievous glint in her eye. "I don't know. Are you sure you can handle training me? I might just surprise you with my natural talent."

I laugh, remembering her determination during our axe-throwing lesson. "Oh, I'm counting on it, my love. I'm counting on it."

We sit there, planning out her training schedule

and discussing the challenges ahead, and I hold her close, feeling her warmth against me. No matter the threat, I will do everything in my power to keep her safe. Not just because she's my mate, or the future queen of our clan. But because she's Luciana, the woman who brought light and love back into my life when I thought all hope was lost.

4

THE LAWS OF COMBAT

The early morning light filters through the frosted windows of the training room, casting long shadows across the padded floor. The air is crisp with the scent of leather and pine, a familiar aroma that speaks of countless hours of practice and dedication. I stand in the center, watching as Luciana enters, her eyes still heavy with sleep but burning with determination. She's dressed in form-fitting training gear, her hair pulled back in a tight braid that swings with each step.

"Good morning, my love," I say, unable to keep the pride from my voice. "Ready to begin?"

She nods, stifling a yawn. "As ready as I'll ever be. Though I have to say, I'm not sure I'll ever get used to these early morning starts."

I chuckle, moving to meet her. The floorboards creak softly under my feet, a reminder of the age and history of this room where generations of Alexeevs have honed their skills. "The early bear catches the... well, whatever it is bears catch."

Luciana rolls her eyes, but I can see the smile tugging at her lips. "I'm pretty sure that's not how the saying goes."

"Details, details," I wave off her comment, then grow serious. I place my hands on her shoulders, feeling the tension in her muscles. "Now, before we begin, I want you to understand something. Training with me will be a challenge. I won't go easy on you just because you're my mate."

She straightens, her chin lifting in defiance. "Good. I don't want you to."

Pride swells in my chest at her words. "That's my girl. Now, let's start with some basic stances."

For the next hour, I guide Luciana through a series of defensive postures and blocks. My hands ghost over her body, adjusting her stance here, her arm position there. Each touch sends a small thrill through me, reminding me of the strength of our connection. She's a quick study, her body adapting to the movements with a grace that never fails to impress me. But I can see the frustration building in her eyes as we repeat the same motions over and over.

"Gavriil," she says finally, wiping sweat from her brow, "when are we going to get to the actual fighting?"

I raise an eyebrow. "Eager to throw a punch, are we?"

She flushes slightly but doesn't back down. Her hands clench at her sides, a telltale sign of her determination. "I just... I want to be prepared. If there really are rogue shifters out there, I need to know how to defend myself."

The reminder of the threat looming over us sends a chill down my spine. Images of blood-soaked battles flash through my mind, memories I've tried hard to suppress. I move closer, cupping her face in my hands. "And you *will* be. But defense is just as important as offense, love. These basics could save your life one day."

Luciana nods, leaning into my touch. "I know. I'm sorry, I'm just..."

"Frustrated?" I finish for her. "It's understandable. But trust me, okay? I won't let anything happen to you."

She looks up at me, her hazel eyes filled with love and determination. "I know you won't. But I want to be able to protect myself, too. And you, if it comes to that."

My heart swells at her words. "Alright then," I say, stepping back and assuming a fighting stance. "Show me what you've got."

What follows is a flurry of movement, Luciana putting everything she's learned so far into practice. She's not as strong as a shifter, of course, but what she lacks in raw power she makes up for in speed and agility.

As we spar, I'm captivated by the fire in her eyes, the way she throws herself into each movement with total commitment. She may be human, but in this moment, she's every bit as fierce as any bear in my clan.

Finally, after a particularly impressive series of blocks and counterattacks, I call a halt. Luciana stands before me, chest heaving, a triumphant grin on her face.

"How was that?" she asks, slightly out of breath.

I smile, pulling her into my arms. "That, my love, was incredible. You're a natural."

She beams up at me, her cheeks flushed with exertion and pride. "Really? You're not just saying that because you have to?"

I laugh, pressing a kiss to her forehead. "When

have you ever known me to say something I don't mean?"

"Fair point," she concedes, then winces slightly as she shifts in my arms.

Concern immediately floods through me. "Are you alright? Did I hurt you?"

Luciana shakes her head, but I can see the discomfort in her eyes. "Just a bit sore. I guess I'm using muscles I didn't even know I had."

I frown, guilt gnawing at me. "Perhaps we should call it a day. We can pick up again tomorrow when you've had a chance to rest."

But Luciana straightens, a stubborn set to her jaw that I've come to know well. "No. I can keep going. I need to be ready, Gavriil. For whatever's coming."

I study her for a moment, torn between admiration for her determination and concern for her well-being. Finally, I nod. "Alright. But we'll take it easier for the rest of the session. And afterwards, I'm running you a hot bath. Non-negotiable."

She grins, rising on her toes to press a quick kiss to my lips. "Deal. Now, what's next?"

We spend the next hour working on grappling techniques, my hands guiding her through the motions. It's an intimate form of training, our bodies pressed close as I show her how to break holds and escape from various grips.

As we move together, I find myself excruciatingly aware of every point of contact between us. The scent of her skin, the warmth of her body against mine, the softness of her hair brushing my cheek... it's intoxicating.

Luciana must sense the change in my demeanor because she pauses, looking up at me with a knowing smile. "Focus, Your Majesty," she teases. "I thought you said you wouldn't go easy on me."

I growl playfully, tightening my hold on her. "Oh, I'm focused alright. Just not on training anymore."

She laughs, the sound echoing through the training room. "Down, boy. We're supposed to be working, remember?"

With great reluctance, I release her, stepping back to put some distance between us. "You're right, of course. Though I must say, you're making it *very* difficult to concentrate."

Luciana's eyes sparkle with mischief. "Oh? And here I thought the great Ursa King was above such distractions."

I raise an eyebrow, a challenge in my voice. "Really? Well then, perhaps it's time I showed you just how... focused I can be."

What follows is the most intense training session yet. I push Luciana to her limits, testing her endurance, her reflexes, her ability to think on her feet. And to my immense pride and amazement, she meets every demand, surpassing my expectations at every turn.

By the time we finish, we're both breathing heavily, sweat glistening on our skin. Luciana stands before me, her hair a wild tangle around her face, her eyes bright with exertion and triumph.

"Well?" she asks, a hint of cockiness in her voice. "How was that for focus?"

I can't stop the grin that spreads across my face. "That, my love, was absolutely incredible."

She beams at the praise, then winces as she stretches out her shoulders. "I think I'm going to be feeling this for days."

"Come here," I say, moving behind her. Gently, I massage her shoulders, working out the knots of tension.

Luciana sighs, leaning back into my touch. "That feels amazing," she murmurs.

As my hands work their way down her back, I marvel at the strength I feel beneath her skin. She may be human, but there's a core of steel in this woman that is simply astonishing. A low growl rumbles in my chest.

"I know what that sound means," Luciana says, tilting her head to look up at me. "But I'd rather hear you say it with words."

I smile, pressing a kiss to the top of her head. "You are incredible. I'm so proud of you."

She turns in my arms, wrapping her own around my waist. "I couldn't do any of this without you, you know. Your support, your belief in me... it means everything."

My heart swells with love for this remarkable woman. "You give me far too much credit, my love. This strength, this determination... it's all you. I'm just lucky enough to be along for the ride."

Luciana rises up on her toes, pressing a soft kiss to my lips. "We're in this together, remember? Partners in everything."

I nod, tightening my hold on her. "Partners. Always."

As we stand there, holding each other in the quiet of the training room, I'm struck once again by how perfectly we fit together. Not just physically, but in every way that matters.

"Come on," I say finally, reluctantly loosening my hold on her. "Let's get you that hot bath I promised.

And then, if you're up for it, perhaps we can explore some... *alternative* forms of physical activity."

Luciana laughs, her eyes twinkling with mischief. "Why, Your Majesty. Are you propositioning me?"

I grin, scooping her up into my arms. "Always, my love. Always."

As I carry her out of the training room, her laughter echoing through the halls of our home, I'm filled with a sense of rightness, of completeness. This is where we belong. Together.

5

SURPRISE, SURPRISE

The grand Alexeev estate stands silent in the pre-dawn chill of Saint Petersburg, its imposing facade softened by a fresh blanket of snow. Inside, the halls are hushed, save for the occasional creak of ancient floorboards as I make my way through the shadowy corridors. My footsteps are purposefully light; today of all days, I can't risk waking Luciana too early.

I pause at the door to our chambers, my hand resting on the ornate handle. Beyond this threshold lies the woman who has transformed my world, still peacefully unaware that today marks her birthday. A smile tugs at my lips as I think of the surprises that await her. With one last steadying breath, I push open the door and step into our room.

Luciana sleeps soundly, her golden hair spread across the pillow, her face serene in the soft light of dawn filtering through the frost-laced windows. I've let her believe that today will be filled with more training, another step in her journey to becoming my Ursa Queen. Little does she know, I have something entirely different planned.

As if sensing my presence, Luciana stirs, her eyes fluttering open. A sleepy smile spreads across her face as she focuses on me. "Доброе утро," she murmurs, her Russian still adorably accented.

"Morning, my love," I reply, leaning in to press a soft kiss to her lips. "Sleep well?"

She nods, stretching languidly. The covers slip down, revealing the curve of her shoulder, and I resist the urge to trace it with my fingers. "Mmm, like a bear in hibernation. Though I have to say, I'm a bit nervous about what you have planned for today's training session. It's always a surprise with you."

I chuckle, playing along with her assumption. "Well, we can't have you getting too comfortable, can we? An Ursa Queen needs to be prepared for anything."

Luciana groans, burying her face in the pillow. "It's too early for your cryptic king speak. Can't we just stay in bed a little longer?"

For a moment, I'm tempted. The sight of her, sleep-tousled and warm, is almost too much to resist. But I have a schedule to keep if everything is going to be ready in time. "As tempting as that is, we have a lot to cover today. Up and at 'em, my future queen."

She throws me a mock glare as she reluctantly sits up. "You're lucky I love you, you know that?"

I grin, pulling her in for another quick kiss. "Believe me, I know. Now, get dressed. I'll meet you downstairs for breakfast in fifteen minutes."

As I make my way to the kitchen, a thrill of excitement rushes through me. I've been planning this surprise for weeks, coordinating with Natalya and Sasha to ensure everything goes smoothly. And the crowning jewel of it all—a very special guest's presence—was a logistical nightmare.

I'm finishing up a batch of blini when Luciana enters the kitchen, dressed in comfortable training clothes. Her eyes widen as she takes in the spread on the table—a feast fit for royalty, with every Russian delicacy I know she loves.

Plates of thinly sliced kolbasa, its rich, smoky aroma mingling with the scent of perfectly scrambled eggs, sit alongside a steaming platter of golden-brown pirozhki, their flaky crusts barely containing the savory meat filling within. A bowl of creamy tvorog, its soft white curds glistening in the morning light, is garnished with fresh berries and a drizzle of honey. The blini, still warm from the pan, are stacked high, ready to be adorned with an assortment of sweet and savory toppings.

"Wow," she says, her eyes roaming over the lavish spread, "you went all out this morning. What's the occasion?"

I shrug, keeping my expression neutral. "Can't a man spoil his mate without an occasion?"

She narrows her eyes suspiciously but doesn't press the issue, instead digging into the feast before her with gusto. As we eat, I outline the day's "training schedule," carefully crafted to keep her occupied and away from the party preparations happening behind the scenes.

"We'll start with a run through the winter gardens," I explain between bites. "Then some wilderness survival skills—you never know when you might need to start a fire in the snow. After lunch, we'll work on your tracking abilities."

Luciana nods, her expression a mix of determination and resignation. "Sounds... intense. But I guess that's the point, right?"

I reach across the table to squeeze her hand.

"You're doing excepcionally well, you know. I couldn't be prouder of how far you've come."

Her cheeks flush with pleasure at the praise.

After breakfast, we bundle up against the cold and head out into the crisp morning air. The estate's winter gardens are a wonderland, the glass domes encasing a variety of plants from around the world. As we jog along the winding paths, I notice how easily Luciana keeps pace with me now. The training is paying off, building her endurance and strength day by day.

We pause at a clearing, Luciana's breath coming out in puffs of white in the cold air. "Okay," she says, hands on her knees as she catches her breath. "What's next, oh wise teacher?"

I grin, gesturing to the pristine snow around us. "Now, we learn how to start a fire in less-than-ideal conditions. Essential survival skill for any member of the Ursa Clan."

For the next hour, I guide Luciana through the process of gathering dry tinder from beneath the snow, showing her how to create a spark using flint and steel. Her first few attempts are unsuccessful, frustration evident in the set of her shoulders.

"I don't understand," she mutters, striking the flint again and again. "Why isn't it working?"

I move behind her, covering her delicate hands with my own. "Like this," I murmur, guiding her movements. "It's all in the angle and the force."

Together, we create a shower of sparks that catch the tinder, a small flame springing to life. Luciana's face lights up with triumph. "I did it!"

"You did," I agree, pressing a kiss to her temple. "Well done, my love."

As the morning wears on, I lead Luciana through a series of wilderness exercises, all carefully designed to keep her occupied and unaware of the preparations happening back at the house. By the time we break for lunch—a picnic I've packed, complete with thermoses of hot cocoa—she's flushed with exertion and pride in her accomplishments.

"I have to admit," she says between bites of sandwiches, "this isn't quite the grueling training session I was expecting. It's actually been... fun."

I chuckle, reaching out to brush a stray lock of hair from her face. "Who says training can't be enjoyable? Besides, these are all valuable skills for a future queen to have. And you will make an extraordinary queen."

Luciana rolls her eyes, but I can see the smile tugging at her lips. She leans into my touch. "Flatterer."

After lunch, we move on to tracking exercises. I lead Luciana through the basics of reading signs in the snow and underbrush, showing her how to identify different animal tracks and what they can tell us about their behaviors.

As the afternoon wears on, I keep a careful eye on the time. Everything needs to be timed perfectly for the surprise to work. Finally, as the sun begins to dip towards the horizon, painting the sky in hues of pink and gold, I suggest we head back to the house.

"Already?" Luciana asks, surprise evident in her voice. "I thought we'd be out here until dark."

I shrug, feigning nonchalance. "We've covered a lot of ground today. Besides, I thought you might appreciate a hot shower and a warm meal after all this outdoor activity."

She eyes me suspiciously but doesn't argue, falling into step beside me as we make our way back through the snow-covered grounds. As we approach the house, I can sense her growing curiosity at my increasingly tense demeanor.

"Gavriil," she says slowly, "what's going on? You're acting strange."

I squeeze her hand reassuringly. "Nothing's wrong, I promise. Just... trust me, okay?"

She nods, though I can see the questions burning

in her eyes. As we reach the front door of the house, I pause, turning to face her.

"Before we go in," I say, my heart racing with anticipation, "I need you to close your eyes."

Luciana's eyebrows shoot up. "What? Why?"

"Please," I breathe. "Just… humor me."

With a sigh that's equal parts exasperation and fondness, she complies, her eyes fluttering shut. I take her hand, carefully guiding her through the door and into the main hall of the house.

The scene that greets us is exactly as I'd hoped. The room has been transformed, decorated with twinkling lights and colorful streamers. A banner hangs across the far wall, proclaiming "Happy Birthday Luciana!" in bold letters. And gathered in the center of the room, barely containing their excitement, are our friends and family.

I position Luciana in the middle of the room, then lean in close to whisper in her ear. "Okay, you can open your eyes now."

The moment she does, the room erupts in a chorus of "Surprise!"

Luciana gasps, her hands flying to her mouth as she takes in the scene before her. I see tears welling in her eyes as she spots familiar faces—Natalya, Sasha,

Dima and Mila, Vlad and Samara—all grinning widely.

But it's the figure stepping out from behind the others that truly catches her attention. Marco, looking slightly overwhelmed but undeniably happy, opens his arms wide. "Happy birthday, *cara*!"

"Marco!" Luciana cries, rushing forward to throw herself into her best friend's arms. "How—what—I can't believe you're here!"

I hang back, watching with a heart full of joy as Luciana embraces Marco, then turns to hug each of our friends. When she finally makes her way back to me, her eyes are shining with unshed tears.

"You did all this?" she asks, her voice thick with emotion. "For me?"

I pull her close, pressing a kiss to her forehead. "Of course. Happy birthday, baby."

She buries her face in my chest, and I can feel her trembling slightly. "I thought you'd forgotten," she mumbles against my shirt.

"Never," I promise, tightening my arms around her. "I could never forget, Luciana."

When she pulls back, her smile is radiant. "Thank you," she says softly. "This is... it's perfect."

As the party unfolds around us, a sense of

profound contentment washes over me. This, I realize, is what I've been fighting for all along. Not just the safety of my clan or the preservation of our way of life, but moments like these—filled with laughter, love, and the warmth of family and friends.

6

THE PARTY

The party that follows is everything I'd hoped it would be. Our home is filled with laughter and warmth as we eat, drink, and celebrate.

The air is thick with the mingled aromas of savory roasted meats, sweet pastries, and the sharp tang of vodka. Glasses clink merrily, and the hum of conversation is punctuated by bursts of laughter. The warmth from the fireplace and the press of bodies makes the room cozy, a stark contrast to the frigid night outside.

As the evening progresses, Luciana catches my eye from across the room. She leans in close, her breath warm against my ear. "I'm going to change into something more... festive," she whispers, a mischievous glint in her eye. "I'll be back soon."

When she returns a short while later, my breath catches in my throat. She's traded her sportswear for a stunning deep red dress that hugs her curves perfectly. The silky fabric shimmers in the firelight, bringing out the golden highlights in her hair. She's let her hair down, too, soft waves framing her face.

As she rejoins the party, accepting compliments with a gracious smile, I find myself counting the minutes until we can be alone.

The celebration continues in full swing, the room alive with joy and camaraderie. I force myself to focus on our guests, to be the gracious host, even as my gaze keeps drifting back to Luciana. She moves through the crowd with effortless charm, her laughter a melody that calls to me above the din of the gathering.

Natalya has outdone herself with the food, a fusion of Russian and Italian cuisines that has everyone raving. Samara leads us in traditional Ursa Clan birthday songs, her clear voice ringing out above the others.

Throughout it all, Luciana glows with happiness. She moves from group to group, chatting animatedly with our friends, but always returning to

Marco's side, as if to reassure herself that he's really here.

As the night wears on, I find myself in a quiet corner with Sasha, watching as Luciana teaches Marco and Dima some Italian drinking game.

"You did well," Sasha says, clapping me on the shoulder. "I don't think I've ever seen her this happy."

I nod, unable to take my eyes off Luciana. "It wasn't easy, keeping it all a secret. Especially getting Marco here without her finding out."

Sasha chuckles. "Yes, well, smuggling the human into Russia under the nose of the lingering vampire covens wasn't exactly a walk in the park. But it was worth it, seeing her face light up like that."

"Thank you," I say sincerely, turning to face my friend and enforcer. "For everything. I couldn't have pulled this off without you."

He waves off my gratitude with a smile. "It's what family does, Your Majesty. Besides, Luciana has become dear to all of us. She deserves this happiness."

As if sensing our attention, Luciana looks up, her eyes meeting mine across the room. The love I see shining there takes my breath away. She excuses herself from her game, making her way over to us.

"What are you two plotting over here?" she asks teasingly as she slips her arm around my waist.

I pull her close, pressing a kiss to her temple. "No plotting, I promise. Just admiring the birthday girl."

Luciana blushes, ducking her head. "I still can't believe you did all this. And Marco! How on earth did you manage that? He told me he couldn't even get a passport."

Sasha and I exchange a look, remembering the bureaucratic nightmare we navigated. "Well… it might have involved a lot of planning, a few bribes, and possibly bending a law or two," Sasha says with a wink.

Luciana's eyes widen. "You didn't!"

I chuckle, shaking my head. "Nothing too nefarious, I assure you. Marco's passport situation was… complicated. Years of never leaving Rome left him without the proper documentation. We simply… expedited the process."

"Expedited?" Luciana raises an eyebrow, clearly not buying it.

"Let's just say some officials in the Italian passport office suddenly found themselves highly *motivated* to clear a backlog of applications," Sasha adds with a grin. "And our contacts at the Russian embassy were remarkably efficient in processing his visa."

I laugh, shaking my head. "Don't worry, love. Everything was perfectly legal… Mostly."

She swats my arm playfully. "You're terrible, you know that? Both of you."

"And yet you love us anyway," I tease.

Her expression softens, her eyes filled with warmth as she looks between Sasha and me. "I do. So much. Thank you, both of you, for everything."

Sasha clears his throat, clearly uncomfortable with the emotional turn of the conversation. "Yes, well, I should go make sure Dima hasn't drunk all the vodka. Enjoy your evening, Your Majesties."

As he walks away, Luciana turns to me, her expression curious. "*Your Majesties?* Plural?"

I shrug, trying to appear nonchalant even as my heart races. "Well, you *are* the future queen. It's only natural that they start thinking of you that way."

She studies me for a moment, her gaze thoughtful. "Gavriil... are you planning something?"

I raise an eyebrow, the picture of innocence. "Planning? Me? Whatever gave you that idea?"

Luciana narrows her eyes suspiciously, but before she can press further, Natalya calls for everyone's attention. "Time for cake!" she announces, wheeling out an enormous confection covered in candles.

As our friends gather around, singing another round of birthday songs, I watch Luciana's face, illuminated by the warm glow of the candles. She looks around the room, taking in the faces of those gathered here to celebrate her, and I can see the moment it truly hits her—this is her family now, her home.

When the song ends, she closes her eyes for a moment, then blows out the candles in one big breath. The sweet scent of extinguished candles mingles with the rich aroma of chocolate frosting. As Natalya cuts into the cake, the moist layers yield easily, releasing a wave of vanilla and cocoa that makes my mouth water.

Everyone cheers, and as Natalya begins cutting and distributing slices of cake, I pull Luciana aside. "Having a good time?" I ask softly, brushing a stray lock of hair behind her ear.

She nods, her eyes shining. "The best. I can't remember the last time I celebrated my birthday like this. Probably not since before my grandfather passed."

My heart aches at the hint of sadness in her voice. "Well, get used to it. Because as long as I'm around, every birthday will be a grand celebration."

Luciana rises on her toes, pressing a soft kiss to my lips. "You're the best boyfriend ever, you know that? The best."

"Save your praise until bedtime," I murmur

against her lips. "I've planned something *quite* special."

We're interrupted by Marco, who approaches with a mischievous grin. "Sorry to break up the love fest," he says, not sounding sorry at all, "but I was promised embarrassing stories about my best friend's adventures in *Shifterland*. Who do I talk to for those?"

Luciana groans, burying her face in my chest. "No one. Absolutely no one."

I laugh, nuzzling her towards Marco. "Go on, love. Catch up with your friend. I'm sure Samara would be more than happy to regale him with tales of your... less graceful moments."

She throws me a mock glare as Marco leads her away, but I can see the happiness radiating from her. Watching her laugh and joke with Marco, surrounded by our Ursa family, Luciana continues to amaze me with how effortlessly she fits in this world.

As the night wears on, the party shows no signs of slowing down. Dima challenges Marco to a drinking contest, which Natalya wisely puts a stop to before it can get out of hand. Samara leads an impromptu dance lesson, teaching Luciana and Marco traditional Ursa Clan steps.

Through it all, I can't take my eyes off Luciana.

She's radiant, her cheeks flushed with happiness and maybe a bit too much wine. Every so often, her gaze finds mine across the room, and the love I see there takes my breath away.

Finally, as the hour grows late and our guests begin to tire, I decide it's time for the final surprise of the evening. I move towards Luciana's side, gently pulling her away from her conversation with Natalya.

"Can I steal you away for a moment?" I ask, my heart pounding with anticipation.

She nods, curiosity evident in her eyes as I lead her out onto the balcony. The night air is crisp and cold, our breath forming little clouds in front of us. Above, the sky is a riot of stars, more brilliant than any I've seen in a long time.

"Gavriil, what—?" Luciana begins, but I silence her with a gentle finger to her lips.

"Just wait," I say softly, pulling her close.

For a moment, all is quiet save for the soft sounds of the party inside and the gentle rustling of wind through the trees. Then, suddenly, the sky explodes with color.

Luciana gasps as the first fireworks burst overhead, painting the night in shades of red and gold. "Oh, Gavriil," she breathes, her eyes wide with wonder. "It's beautiful."

I wrap my arms around her from behind, resting my chin on her shoulder as we watch the spectacle unfold. "Not as beautiful as you," I murmur in her ear.

She turns in my arms, her eyes shining with emotion. "You are... incredible, you know that? I can't believe you did all this for me."

"I'd do anything for you, Luciana," I say softly, cupping her face in my hands. "You've brought so much light into my life, so much joy. I want to spend every day making you as happy as you've made me."

Her breath catches, and I can see the realization dawning in her eyes. "Gavriil..." she whispers.

Slowly, never taking my eyes from hers, I sink down to one knee. I can hear gasps and excited murmurs from inside as our friends realize what's happening, but in this moment, there's only Luciana.

"Luciana Marino," I begin, my voice steady despite the nerves fluttering in my stomach. "From the moment I met you, my life changed. You challenged me, surprised me, made me laugh in a way I hadn't in years. You've faced every obstacle thrown your way with courage and grace, embracing this world of ours with an open heart and mind."

I reach into my pocket, pulling out a small velvet box. Inside is a ring, an heirloom passed down through generations of Ursa royalty. The central stone is a rare blue diamond, surrounded by smaller white diamonds set in a pattern reminiscent of a bear's paw print.

"You are my heart, my home, my everything," I continue, my voice trembling slightly as I open the box to reveal the ring. My heart pounds so fiercely I fear it might burst from my chest, and my mouth feels as dry as the Sahara.

I take a shaky breath, my eyes never leaving Luciana's. "I want to spend the rest of my life by your side." My voice grows stronger with each word, fueled by the depth of my love for this extraordinary woman. "Will you do me the honor of becoming my wife, my queen, my partner in all things?"

My hands tremble slightly as I hold the ring out to her. The words hang in the air between us, filled with promise and hope. I feel as if I'm standing on the edge of a precipice, my entire future balanced on her answer.

Tears are streaming down Luciana's face now, but her smile is radiant. For a heart-stopping moment, she's silent, and I feel a flicker of doubt. But then she's nodding, laughing through her tears.

"Yes," she says, her voice thick with emotion.

"Yes, of course I'll marry you, you wonderful, impossible man."

Relief and joy surge through me as I slip the ring onto her finger. It fits perfectly, as if it were always meant to be there. I stand, pulling Luciana into my arms and kissing her deeply, pouring all my love and happiness into the gesture.

The balcony erupts in cheers and applause, and I realize dimly that our entire party has spilled out to witness the moment. But I only have eyes for Luciana, my fiancée, my future queen.

When we finally break apart, both breathless and grinning like fools, we're immediately swarmed by our friends. There are hugs and congratulations, tears and laughter. Marco pulls Luciana into a fierce embrace, whispering something in her ear that makes her laugh through her tears.

Vladimir approaches, his usual stoic demeanor softened by a rare, genuine smile. He claps me on the shoulder, his grip firm and brotherly. "Congratulations, brother," he says, his voice gruff with emotion. "I wish you all the joy."

Samara follows close behind, her eyes shining with unshed tears. She embraces both Luciana and me in a tight hug. "I always knew you two were meant for each other," she says warmly. "Welcome to the family, sister."

The party, which had been winding down, surges back to life with renewed energy. Sasha produces several bottles of champagne from somewhere, and soon everyone has a glass in hand.

"A toast!" Dima calls out, raising his glass high. "To Gavriil and Luciana, our king and future queen. May their reign be long and prosperous, and may their love shine as bright as the stars above us."

"To Gavriil and Luciana!" everyone echoes, glasses clinking.

As the celebration continues around us, I pull Luciana close once more. "Happy birthday, my love," I murmur against her hair.

She looks up at me, her eyes shining with joy and love. "Best birthday ever," she says, rising on her toes to kiss me again.

The party lasts well into the early hours of the morning. There's more dancing, more drinking, more laughter than I can remember in years. Through it all, Luciana never strays far from my side, her hand constantly seeking mine, as if to reassure herself that this is all real.

Finally, as the sky lightens with the first hints of

dawn, our guests begin to depart. There are more hugs, more congratulations, promises to celebrate again soon.

Marco pulls Luciana into one final, fierce embrace. "I'm so happy for you, *cara*," he says, his voice thick with emotion. "You deserve all of this and more."

Luciana sniffs, wiping away a stray tear. "Thank you for being here, Marco. It means more than you know."

Marco pulls back, his hands resting on Luciana's shoulders as he grins. "Well, get used to having me around. I'll be staying here for at least a week, so we should make some plans soon. I want to see everything this frozen wonderland has to offer."

His enthusiasm amuses me, so reminiscent of Luciana's when she first arrived. I chuckle, and the sound draws their attention, and her eyes meet mine, sparkling with joy.

"I'm sure we can arrange a tour," I say, stepping closer to wrap an arm around Luciana's waist. "Though I must warn you, Marco, Saint Petersburg in winter is not for the faint of heart."

Luciana laughs, the sound warming me more thoroughly than any fire. "Don't worry, I'll make sure you're properly bundled up, Marco. We can't have you turning into an icicle before the week is out."

With final hugs and promises to meet soon, Marco takes his leave, the last of our guests to depart.

As the heavy oak door closes with a soft thud, the party's lively atmosphere seems to dissipate. The clink of glasses and the hum of conversation fade, replaced by the subtle tick of the grandfather clock and the gentle crackle of the dying fire. The sudden absence of noise presses against my ears, a tangible shift in the air.

Luciana turns to me, exhaustion and happiness warring on her face. "That was..."

"Overwhelming?" I suggest, pulling her into my arms.

She nods, resting her head on my chest. "But in the *best* possible way. I can't believe this is real."

I tilt her chin up, meeting her gaze. "Believe it, my love. This is just the beginning."

Luciana's eyes sparkle with mischief. "The beginning, hm? And what happens next, Your Majesty?"

In answer, I scoop her up into my arms, delighting in her surprised laugh. "Next, my queen, we celebrate. *Privately.*"

As I carry her towards our bedroom, Luciana's arms around my neck and her laughter ringing in my ears, I'm filled with a sense of rightness, of completeness.

I lay her down on our four-poster bed, adorned with satin sheets and plush pillows, the soft predawn light casting a warm, inviting glow across her skin. I cannot help but marvel at my fortune. This vibrant, passionate woman is mine, forever. Leaning in, I brush feather-light kisses along her jawline, eliciting delicious shivers from her.

"Tell me," she whispers between gasps, "tell me again how much you love me."

Gazing into her hazel eyes, I cradle her face in my hands. "Luciana... words cannot do justice to the depth of my feelings for you. You're the very air I breathe, the rhythm in my heartbeat. Without you, I am lost."

Her eyes brim with tears once more, but this time they are tears of joy. "And I love you, my future husband. So much that it scares me sometimes." She traces a finger along my jawline.

"I never thought I'd find someone who could accept all of me," I breathe, "magic and all."

"Ah, but that's why I adore you," she teases, gently gliding her hand along my firm jawline. "You're a wonderful man—your magical abilities are just one more reason to love you."

A playful smile tugs at my lips. "Well, if you insist..." In an instant, a shower of rose petals rains down upon us, their sweet scent permeating the air. The enchanted music of a hundred instruments begins to play softly in the background as we surrender to our passions.

"Luciana," I whisper, my voice rough with emotion and desire. The sight of her, bathed in pale morning light and rose petals, steals the breath from my lungs. Words feel inadequate in this moment, but I try anyway. "I want to remember every second of this. Every touch, every breath." My hand cups her cheek, thumb tracing her lower lip. "You are every-thing to me."

Cradling her face in my hands, I press a searing kiss to her soft lips, tasting the sweet nectar of her love and devotion. Her response is immediate and fervent, her arms wrapping around my neck as if she were a vine entwined with her beloved oak. Our mouths find each other gently, our tongues inter-twining seductively to the beat of our racing hearts.

Yielding to the intoxicating heat between us, I reluctantly break our kiss, my hands sliding to the zipper at the back of her dress. With trembling fingers, I slowly lower it, the soft rasp of metal on metal seeming impossibly loud in the quiet room.

The silky fabric parts, revealing a tantalizing glimpse of bare skin.

I ease the straps off her shoulders, pressing soft kisses to each newly exposed inch. The red dress, which has captivated me all evening, now slips away as I gently tug it down her body. I pull it free, letting it fall to the floor beside the bed in a crimson puddle. The sight of her naked form, bathed in the pale glow of predawn light filtering through the windows, steals the breath from my lungs.

Propping myself up on one elbow, I trail my free hand up the smooth expanse of her legs, reveling in the softness of her skin. My lips follow, leaving a trail of heated kisses along her thighs, her hips, her stomach. As I reach her collarbone, I pause, looking up to meet her gaze. The love and desire I see reflected there matches my own, spurring me on.

I lavish attention on the sensitive skin of her neck, savoring every quiver and soft moan that escapes her parted lips. Her fingers tangle in my hair, urging me closer, and I'm all too happy to oblige.

Luciana's scent is a heady blend of rosewater and womanly desire that threatens to consume me whole. Her skin is softer than the petals falling around us, her curves a symphony of perfection that inflames my senses to fever pitch. As I trace my tongue along the valley between her breasts, she arches her back in supplication, offering herself willingly to my ministrations.

I tease her hardened nipple with the softest of touches, reveling in the pleasure it brings her. Her fingers tangle in my hair as she moans against me, her body arching towards the sensations I elicit. I draw her taut peak into my mouth, suckling gently at first, then with increasing fervor as her moans spur me on. At the same time, my fingertips trail down her stomach, tracing the contours of her abdomen and stopping just short of the center of her arousal. Luciana whimpers, her hips twisting in silent supplication.

Catching her eye, I trace a single finger along her damp folds, and she gasps, her cheeks flushing a deep shade of crimson. Shyly, she diverts her gaze but doesn't stop me as I continue to explore her slick heat. Slowly, I part the delicate petals of her womanhood, inhaling the musky scent of her arousal before dipping my tongue tentatively between the delicate folds.

Luciana's reaction is immediate and potent. With a cry, she throws back her head as stars dance in her eyes. Encouraged by the intensity of sensation coursing through her body, I continue to lavish attention on every sensitive inch of her most private domain. Flicking my tongue over her swollen bud, I delight in the way she grinds against my face in desperate seek of more.

"Gavriil," she pants, "I... I can't..." Her words trail off into a strangled moan as I slip two fingers inside of her warmth, curling them in an age-old rhythm that I know will send her over the edge.

Arching like a bow under my ministrations, Luciana's nails dig into the soft satin beneath her, her body shuddering with building pleasure. The sight of her, lost in the throes of ecstasy, is enough to make my need nearly unbearable. Carefully, I withdraw my fingers and crawl up her trembling form, my manhood aching for her. With a tenderness born of bliss, I position myself at her entrance and gaze into her eyes.

Her pupils are wide with desire, irises nearly swallowed in their depths. She nods, wordlessly allowing me to take what is already mine. Taking a shuddering breath, I push forward, sheathing myself inside of her warmth inch by agonizingly slow inch.

Luciana gasps, her hips bucking against mine as I fill her completely. The sensation of our bodies joined as one is indescribable; it's as if the world is made anew in that very moment, created solely for the two of us.

Her inner muscles clamp down around my length like a velvet vice, squeezing me in a tight grip that sends shivers down my spine. Groaning, I pull back only to thrust forward again, setting a steady rhythm that has us both panting for air in no time at all.

"Tell me you're mine," I growl, my voice hoarse with untamed desire. "Say it."

Breathless, she gasps out the words I crave. "Yours," she says, her hands caressing my face. "All yours."

The admission ignites a primal fire within me, and I lose all inhibitions. I ravage her mouth with a feral hunger as my hips pick up the pace, plunging into her depths with a relentless fervor. Her nails rake down my back, leaving behind trails of delicious pain that only serve to fan the flames of my desire.

As our bodies collide with untamed ferocity, our animalistic sides begin to emerge. My vision is consumed with a golden haze, and I roar as the beast within me struggles to break free. The sound echoes through the room, bouncing off the walls and mingling with Luciana's wanton cries.

Sweat glistens on our entwined bodies, and the scent of our arousal fills the air, musky and intoxicatingly potent. We're no longer man and woman, but alpha bear and mate, driven by instinct alone—

craving to continue our bloodline and solidify our bond.

Luciana's fingers wind themselves in my hair. Her inner walls clamp down around me like a vise as she nears her peak, her body shuddering beneath mine. The feel of her quivering around my length sends me over the edge too, and with one final thrust, I roar our union to the very heavens above. In that moment, it feels as if the whole world pauses—like time itself has stopped just for us two.

As our bodies slowly disentangle, I gather Luciana into my arms, cradling her against my chest. Her skin is flushed and warm, a light sheen of sweat making her glow in the dim light. I brush a stray lock of hair from her face, tucking it gently behind her ear. The simple gesture feels impossibly tender after the intensity of our passion. Luciana looks up at me, her eyes shining with love and contentment, a soft smile playing on her lips. I lean down, pressing a gentle kiss to her forehead, savoring this moment of quiet intimacy.

As the first rays of sunlight loom over the horizon, painting the world in shades of gold and pink, a profound realization settles deep in my core. A promise, unspoken yet binding, forms in my heart. I will love this woman with every fiber of my being, cherishing every moment, embracing every challenge, and celebrating every triumph by her side.

This is more than just a new day dawning; it's the start of a new chapter in our lives. And I, for one, can't wait to see where this journey leads us.

7

I CAN COOK ANYTHING BLINDFOLDED

The kitchen of our Saint Petersburg estate fills with the aroma of sauteing onions and garlic. The sizzle and pop of vegetables hitting the hot oil fills the air, accompanied by the rhythmic sound of Luciana's knife on the cutting board. Steam rises from the pot on the stove, carrying with it the rich scent of simmering herbs and spices.

Luciana stands at the counter, her brow furrowed in concentration as she chops vegetables with painstaking precision. It's impossible for me not to smile when I see how dedicated she is to the task.

"You know," I say, moving behind her, "the vegetables don't have to be perfectly uniform. They'll taste just as good if they're a little misshapen."

Luciana throws me a mock glare over her shoulder. "Easy for you to say, Mr. *I-Can-Cook-Anything-Blindfolded.* Some of us need to focus to avoid chopping off our fingers."

I chuckle, pressing a kiss to the top of her head. "Fair enough. Carry on, my perfectionist queen."

As I move back to the stove to check on the simmering pot, I hear a soft curse behind me. Turning, I see Luciana sucking on her finger, a small drop of blood welling up from a cut.

In an instant, I'm by her side, gently taking her hand in mine. "Let me see," I murmur, examining the small wound.

Luciana rolls her eyes, but there's fondness in her expression. "It's just a nick, Gavriil. I'm not going to bleed out from chopping carrots."

"Humor me," I say, leading her to the sink to rinse the cut. As I carefully dry her hand and apply a small bandage, I'm struck by how domestic this moment is. How normal. It's a far cry from the life I led before Luciana entered my world.

"There," I say, pressing a kiss to her newly bandaged finger. "All better."

Luciana's eyes soften, and she rises on her toes to kiss me properly. "My hero," she teases. "Whatever would I do without you?"

We stand there for a moment, simply enjoying

each other's presence, until the smell of something burning reaches us.

"The bread!" Luciana exclaims, breaking away to rush to the oven.

I can't help but laugh as she pulls out a slightly charred loaf, her face a picture of dismay. "Well," I say, trying to keep a straight face, "I'm sure it's still edible. Mostly."

Luciana swats at me with an oven mitt. "This is your fault, I'll have you know. Distracting me with your... your everything."

I raise an eyebrow, amusement dancing in my eyes. "My *everything*, hm? Care to elaborate on that?"

She blushes, turning back to the counter. "Oh, hush. Help me salvage this meal before we end up having to order takeout. Again."

Still chuckling, I move to her side, taking over the task of chopping vegetables while she attends to the stew. As we work side by side, a comfortable silence falls between us.

"You know," I say after a while, "this reminds me of when I was a child. My mother used to let me help in the kitchen sometimes, on the rare occasions when she cooked herself instead of leaving it to the staff."

Luciana looks up, interest sparking in her eyes. She loves hearing about my childhood, always eager to learn more about the world I come from. "Really? I can't imagine the great Ursa King as a little kitchen helper."

I smile, lost in the memory. "Oh, I was far from great back then. I once managed to spill an entire bag of flour all over myself. Looked like a little ghost running through the halls."

Luciana laughs, the sound warming me more thoroughly than any fire. "Please tell me there are pictures of this somewhere."

"If there are, they're well hidden," I assure her. "But my mother... she didn't get angry. She just laughed and said I looked like a little polar bear cub."

My voice softens as I continue. "She taught me how to make pelmeni that day. Said every good leader should know how to feed themselves and their people."

Luciana's hand finds mine, squeezing gently. "She sounds wonderful. I wish I could have met her."

I bring her hand to my lips, pressing a kiss to her knuckles. "She would have loved you. Probably more than she loved me, if I'm being honest."

We share a smile, the moment tender and bittersweet. Then Luciana's eyes widen. "The stew!" she exclaims, turning back to the pot, which has started to bubble over.

What follows is a flurry of activity as we try to save our dinner. Pots clang, water hisses as it hits the hot stovetop, and the air becomes thick with steam and the complex layering of aromas from our culinary adventure. The rough texture of herbs, the slick feeling of olive oil, and the cool smoothness of vegetables pass through our hands as we work in tandem. Somehow, in the process, I end up with a streak of tomato sauce across my cheek, while Luciana's hair is dusted with herbs.

Finally, we manage to get everything under control. The stew is salvaged, if a bit more reduced than intended, and we even cut away the burnt parts of the bread to create something resembling garlic toast.

As we sit down to eat, I'm filled with wonder as I take in the scene before me. The table is set with our best china, steam rising from the dishes we've prepared together. It's a moment of normalcy in our often chaotic lives, and I savor it to the fullest.

Luciana takes a bite of the stew, her eyes lighting up with pleasure. "Mm… This is delicious," she says. "We make a good team in the kitchen."

I chuckle, reaching for a piece of bread. "Indeed, we do. Though I think your skills with a knife have improved more than your ability to keep an eye on the oven."

She mock glares at me, but I can see the amusement in her eyes. "Very funny, Your Majesty. I'll have you know that bread was perfectly charred."

We share a laugh, but as it fades, I notice a shift in Luciana's demeanor. She pushes her food around her plate, her brow furrowed in thought.

"Gavriil," she says finally, her tone hesitant, "I've been meaning to ask you something about… shifter culture."

I set down my fork, giving her my full attention. "Of course, love. What do you want to know?"

She bites her lip, a sign I've come to recognize as nervousness. "Well, it's about the full moon gatherings. I've noticed that I'm never invited to attend, and I was wondering… is it because I'm human? Am I not *allowed* to be there?"

I frown, caught off guard by the question. "It's not that you're not allowed," I begin, trying to find the right words. "It's just… those gatherings can be intense. Dangerous, even, for humans. Our instincts are stronger during the full moon, harder to control."

Luciana's brow furrows. "But I'm not just any human. I'm your mate, your future queen. Shouldn't I be there, supporting you?"

I sigh, setting down my napkin. "It's complicated, Luciana. Yes, you're my mate, but you're still human. The risk is too great."

"Risk?" she repeats, her voice rising slightly. "What risk? You've claimed me, branded me as yours. Surely that offers some protection?"

I push back from the table, suddenly restless. "It's not that simple. My claim on you is strong, yes, but during the full moon... instincts can override reason. Even with my mark, there's a chance another shifter might..."

I trail off, not wanting to finish the thought. The idea of another shifter trying to claim Luciana, of putting her in that kind of danger, makes my blood run cold.

Luciana stands too, her eyes flashing with a mixture of hurt and anger. "Might what, Gavriil? Attack me? Is that what you think of your own people?"

"No!" I say quickly, annoyed by my inability to make her understand. "It's not about what I think. It's about *instinct*, about the primal nature of shifters that comes out during the full moon."

"So what, I'm just supposed to hide away every full moon for the rest of our lives?" Luciana demands. "How am I supposed to be a proper queen if I'm not allowed to take part in one of the most important rituals of shifter culture?"

I can feel my temper rising, fueled by fear for her safety and frustration at the situation. "This isn't about you being a proper queen," I snap. "This is about *keeping you safe*. Why can't you understand that?"

Luciana recoils as if I've slapped her. "I understand perfectly," she says, her voice cold. "You don't trust me to take care of myself. You still see me as some fragile human who needs to be protected."

"That's not what I meant," I start to say, but she cuts me off.

"I think I need some air," she says, turning towards the door. "I'll be in the garden."

"Baby…" But before I can stop her, she's gone, the door slamming behind her with a finality that makes my heart clench. I slump back into my chair, our half-eaten dinner forgotten. How did this go so wrong so quickly?

I'm still sitting there, replaying the argument in my head and trying to figure out where I went wrong, when a bone-chilling scream pierces the night air.

Luciana.

In an instant, I'm on my feet, racing towards the sound. As I burst out into the garden, the scene that greets me sends ice through my veins. Five massive shapes loom before her, their fur silvered by moonlight. Wolf shifters. Their low growls rumble through the air, a primal sound that sets my teeth on edge. The largest wolf, its eyes gleaming with feral hunger, takes a step forward.

Luciana brandishes a broken tree branch, her knuckles white with the force of her grip. Her chest heaves with rapid breaths, her eyes wide with terror. But there's determination there too, a fierce refusal to give in without a fight.

The scent of fear—Luciana's fear—hits me like a physical blow. It mingles with the wolves' musky odor and the rich, damp smell of the night garden. My muscles tense, ready to spring into action.

Time seems to slow. I see a wolf's haunches bunch, preparing to leap. I hear the whisper of wind through leaves, feel the cool night air on my skin. And beneath it all, the steady, rapid thump of Luciana's heartbeat calls to me.

A growl builds in my chest, rising to a roar that shakes the very ground. The bear within me claws to be released, desperate to protect what's mine. Within seconds, I shift, my bear form erupting in a surge of fur and muscle. I charge at the wolves, my sole thought to protect my mate.

The fight is brutal and swift. Even in their wolf forms, the rogues are no match for an enraged Ursa King. I throw one wolf against a tree with enough force to crack the trunk. Another I catch in my jaws, shaking it like a rag doll before tossing it aside.

Through it all, I'm vaguely aware of shouts and the sounds of more fighting. My Elite team has arrived, drawn by the commotion. *Good.* They can deal with the rest of the pack while I focus on getting Luciana to safety.

As the last wolf falls, I shift back to my human form, rushing to Luciana's side. She's slumped against the wall, her breathing ragged, a nasty gash on her arm where a wolf must have gotten through her defenses.

"Oh gods…" I breathe, gathering her into my arms. "Are you alright, my love? Did they…?"

She shakes her head, clinging to me. "I'm okay," she says, her voice shaky. "You got here in time. You saved me."

Relief washes over me, so strong it nearly brings me to my knees. I hold her tighter, burying my face in her hair and inhaling her scent, reassuring myself that she's really here, really safe.

Around us, the Elite are securing the scene. Two of the wolves lie motionless on the ground, while the others whimper in pain, no longer a threat. Sasha approaches, his expression grim, dragging the pack's leader—now in human form—by the scruff of his neck.

"Your Majesty," Sasha says, his voice low and tense. "We've subdued the attackers. The leader lives, but two didn't survive the fight. What are your orders?"

I look up, still holding Luciana close, my voice cold with barely contained fury. "Take the survivors to the cells. I want the leader under constant guard. We'll interrogate him at dawn."

Sasha nods, his grip tightening on the captured wolf. "And the bodies, sir?"

"Dispose of them," I growl, my eyes flashing with a dangerous glint. "Make sure it sends a message. No one threatens my mate."

Sasha nods, turning to oversee the cleanup. I focus back on Luciana, gently examining her wound. "We need to get you inside, love. Get this looked at."

She nods, allowing me to help her to her feet. As we make our way back to the house, I can feel her trembling against me. The adrenaline is wearing off, the reality of what just happened setting in.

Once inside, I lead her to our bedroom, settling her on the bed while I fetch the first aid kit. As I clean and bandage her wound, neither of us speaks. The tension from our earlier argument still hangs in the air, but it's overshadowed by the weight of what just transpired.

The night's events have left us both shaken, the joy of our earlier domestic bliss now a distant memory. As I finish tending to Luciana's wound, I can't help but wonder how we'll move forward from here. The attack has brought our argument into sharp focus, highlighting the *very real* dangers that come with our life together.

But as I look at Luciana, her face pale but determined, I'm reminded of why I fell in love with her in the first place. Her strength, her resilience, her unwavering commitment to our life together—these are the qualities that make her not just my mate, but my equal.

We have much to discuss, much to work through. But for now, I'm content to hold her close, grateful beyond words that she's safe, and determined to find a way to balance her safety with her rightful place by my side in all aspects of our lives.

8

HEALING OUR WOUNDS

The first rays of dawn are just beginning to streak across the sky as I stand at the window of our bedroom, my gaze unfocused on the frost-covered gardens below. Behind me, Luciana sleeps fitfully, her brow furrowed even in slumber. The events of the night have left their mark on both of us, reopening old wounds and creating new ones.

My mind drifts back to that fateful battle in Rome, the night we faced the vampire coven. The memory of fallen brothers, their bodies strewn across cobblestone streets, hits me with renewed force. The weight of leadership, of responsibility for those lives lost, settles heavily on my shoulders once more.

A soft rustling from the bed draws my attention. Luciana is stirring, her eyes fluttering open. For a moment, confusion clouds her features, then recognition dawns, followed swiftly by concern.

"Gavriil?" she calls softly, pushing herself up to a sitting position. "Are you alright?"

I turn from the window, attempting to school my features into a mask of calm. But Luciana sees right through it, as she always does.

"Come here," she says, patting the space beside her on the bed.

For a moment, I hesitate. The urge to maintain the facade of strength, to be the unshakeable Ursa King, is strong. But the events of the night have left me raw, vulnerable in a way I haven't allowed myself to be in years.

Slowly, I make my way to the bed, sinking down beside Luciana. She immediately wraps her arms around me, pulling me close. I resist for a heartbeat, then allow myself to lean into her embrace, burying my face in the crook of her neck.

"Talk to me," Luciana murmurs, her fingers carding gently through my hair. "What's going on in that head of yours?"

I take a deep, shuddering breath. "I almost lost you," I whisper, the words muffled against her skin. "Just like in Rome. Just like..." I clench my fists, my body trembling with dread and fury. The thought of

Luciana in danger, of her being hurt, ignites a primal anger within me. I should have protected her better, should have anticipated this threat. The bear inside me roars, demanding retribution against those who dared to threaten my mate.

"But you didn't," Luciana says firmly, pulling back to meet my gaze. Her eyes are fierce, determined. "I'm right here, Gavriil. We're *both* here."

I nod, but the knot of fear and guilt in my chest doesn't loosen. "When I saw those wolves surrounding you, all I could think about was Rome. The bodies in the streets, the smell of blood and death. I can't... I can't go through that again, Luciana. I cannot lose you."

Luciana's hand comes up to cup my cheek, her touch achingly gentle. "You won't lose me. We're in this together, remember? Partners in everything?"

Her words, an echo of our earlier conversations, strike a chord within me. I close my eyes, leaning into her touch. "I'm sorry," I murmur. "For earlier. For not listening to you about the full moon gatherings. I was so focused on protecting you that I didn't consider how it made you feel."

"And I'm sorry too," Luciana says softly. "I should have tried to understand your perspective better. I know you're just trying to keep me safe."

I open my eyes, meeting her gaze. "You are the strongest person I know, Luciana. Human or not. I never want you to doubt that. But this world... it's dangerous in ways you're still learning about. The thought of anything happening to you..."

"I understand that now," Luciana nods, her expression serious. "More than ever. But Gavriil... I need you to understand something too. I chose this life, chose *you*, knowing there would be risks. I can't hide away from every danger. We need to find a balance."

I sigh, knowing she's right. "I promise, we'll work on it together. Find a way for you to be involved in all aspects of clan life while still ensuring your safety."

Luciana's smile is soft but determined. "That's all I ask. We're stronger together, Gavriil. Tonight proved that. You saved me, yes, but don't forget—I was holding my own against those wolves before you arrived. Your training is paying off."

Pride swells in my chest at her words, mingling with the lingering fear and guilt. "You were magnificent," I admit, allowing a small smile to tug at my lips. "Terrifying, but magnificent."

Luciana chuckles, the sound easing some of the tension from the air. "Well, I learned from the best.

Now, come here, you big bear. Let me take care of you for a change."

She tugs me down until we're lying side by side, her fingers tracing soothing patterns across my back. I allow myself to relax into her touch, the steady rhythm of her heartbeat a comforting melody in my ears.

"Tell me about Rome," Luciana says after a while, her voice soft in the quiet of the room. "Not just the battle, but... everything. I want to understand."

I take a deep breath, gathering my thoughts. It's not easy to revisit those memories, but I know it's necessary. For both of us.

"The hardest part," I say, my voice rough with emotion, "was facing the families afterwards. Telling them their sons, their brothers, their fathers weren't coming home. That I had failed to protect them."

Luciana's arms tighten around me, but a small wince escapes her as the movement pulls at her bandaged wound. Instantly, I ease her injured arm away, cradling it carefully to prevent further discomfort. My touch is feather-light, while the bear's strength simmers beneath.

Despite the pain, Luciana's eyes remain fixed on mine, filled with unwavering support. "You didn't fail them, Gavriil. You led them into battle, fought along-side them. That's not failure—that's leadership."

I shake my head, unconvinced. "A good leader brings his people home."

"No," Luciana says firmly, pulling back to meet my gaze. "A good leader does everything in his power to protect his people, but understands that some-times, loss is inevitable. You honor their sacrifice by continuing to lead, by protecting those who remain."

Her words strike deep, easing a burden I've carried for far too long. I lean forward, pressing my forehead to hers. "How did you get so wise, hm?" I murmur.

Luciana's smile is soft, tinged with sadness. "I've had my share of loss too, remember? My grandfa-ther... he taught me that grief is the price we pay for love. But it's a price worth paying."

We lapse into silence, each lost in our own thoughts. As the room gradually lightens with the rising sun, I find myself marveling at the woman beside me. Her strength, her compassion, her unwa-vering support—they humble me, make me want to be worthy of the love she offers so freely.

"Luciana," I say softly, breaking the silence. "About the full moon gatherings..."

She looks up at me, curiosity in her eyes.

"I think… I think you should attend the next one," I continue, the words coming slowly as I work through my thoughts. "Not for the entire night, and not without protection. But you're right—you are the future queen of this clan. You should be part of these rituals."

Luciana's face lights up, joy and surprise warring in her expression. "Really? You mean it?"

I nod, resolute despite the fear still churning in my gut. "Yes. We'll take precautions, of course. You'll stay close to me, and we'll have guards nearby. But… you belong there, by my side."

Luciana surges forward, capturing my lips in a fierce kiss. When she pulls back, her eyes are shining with unshed tears. "Thank you," she whispers. "You have no idea how much this means to me." Suddenly, she winces, a sharp "Ow!" escaping her lips as the movement jars her injured arm.

I carefully steady her, concern etched on my face. "You *really* need to be more careful, love," I chide gently, though I can't keep the affection from my voice.

Luciana looks at me sheepishly, then a small giggle bubbles up from her throat. "Guess I got a little carried away with my gratitude," she says, her eyes twinkling with mirth despite the pain.

I can't help but join in her laughter, the sound warm and intimate in the quiet of our room. "What am I going to do with you?" I ask, shaking my head fondly.

"Love me forever?" she suggests, her smile bright and teasing.

I pull her close, mindful of her injury. "Always," I purr against her hair. "That's a promise I'll never have trouble keeping."

I cup her face in my hands, my thumbs brushing away the tears that have spilled over. "I promise, from now on, we face everything together. No more shutting you out, no more making decisions for you. Partners in everything."

Luciana nods, leaning into my touch. "Agreed."

As we lie there, wrapped in each other's arms while the new day dawns outside our window, I feel a sense of peace settling over me. The memories of Rome, the fear from last night's attack—they're still there, but no longer overwhelming.

Last night's events have shaken us, brought old fears to the surface, and created new ones. But they've also strengthened our bond, forced us to confront the realities of our life together and find a way forward.

9

FULL MOON RISING

The anticipation in the air is all but tangible as the sun dips below the horizon, painting the sky in hues of deep orange and purple. I stand on the balcony of our Saint Petersburg estate, watching as the last rays of light fade, giving way to the encroaching darkness. The full moon, a pale ghost in the darkening sky, seems to pulse with an otherworldly energy.

Behind me, I hear the soft rustle of fabric as Luciana joins me. Her delightful scent wraps around me like a comforting blanket. She slips her hand into mine, and I sense the slight tremor in her fingers.

"Are you sure about this?" I ask, turning to face her. The fading light catches the golden highlights in her hair, creating a halo effect that takes my breath away.

Luciana's chin lifts, determination shining in her eyes. "I am," she says, her voice steady despite the nervousness I perceive beneath the surface. "I'm ready, Gavriil."

I study her for a moment, taking in the sight of her. She's dressed in the traditional garb of an Ursa mate attending her first full moon gathering—a flowing gown of deep forest green, embroidered with silver threads that catch the light with every movement.

"Remember," I say, gently squeezing her hand, "stay close to me at all times. If at any point you feel uncomfortable or threatened, just say the word and we'll leave immediately."

She nods, a small smile playing on her lips. "I know, my love. You've only told me about a hundred times since we woke up this morning."

I can't help but chuckle, some of the tension easing from my shoulders. "Can you blame me for being cautious? This is a big step, Luciana. The full moon... it brings out a side of us that can be hard to control."

"I trust you," she says simply, reaching up to cup my cheek. The warmth of her palm against my skin sends a shiver down my spine. "And I trust our people. This is part of who you are, who we are. I want to embrace all of it."

Her words evoke such intense feelings of pride and love in me that it's almost painful. I lean down, capturing her lips in a kiss that's equal parts tender and passionate. When we part, both slightly breathless, I rest my forehead against hers.

"Let's go join our kin," she whispers. "We have a gathering to attend."

With a nod, I take her hand once more and lead her back into our chambers. The room is a flurry of activity as our personal attendants make the final preparations. Sasha stands by the door, his usual stoic expression in place, but I can see the tension in the set of his shoulders.

"Everything is ready, Your Majesty," he says as we approach. "The clan has gathered in the sacred grove. We await only your arrival to begin the ceremony."

I nod, feeling the weight of responsibility settle over me like a cloak. "And the security measures we discussed?"

"In place," Sasha confirms. "Elite guards are stationed at key points around the perimeter. I've instructed them to be as unobtrusive as possible while maintaining vigilance."

"Good," I say, then turn to Luciana. "Are you ready, my love?"

She takes a deep breath, squaring her shoulders. "As I'll ever be."

With that, we make our way through the winding corridors of the estate. An expectant hush has replaced the usual bustle of activity. As we near the main entrance, I can hear the indistinct murmur of voices from outside.

The massive oak doors swing open, and we step out into the cool night air. The full moon now hangs high in the sky, bathing everything in its silvery light. Before us stretches a sea of faces—our clan, gathered to celebrate this most sacred of nights.

A path clears before us as we make our way towards the ancient forest that borders our lands. I can feel the eyes of our people on us, curiosity and excitement mingling with a hint of apprehension. This is the first time a human has been allowed to attend the full moon ritual in living memory.

As we enter the forest, the sounds of the gathered clan fade, replaced by the whisper of wind through leaves and the soft crunch of our footsteps on the forest floor. The air grows thick with the scent of pine and earth, and something else—a wild, primal energy that seems to pulse in time with the beating of my heart.

After what seems like both an eternity and no time at all, we emerge into a moonlit clearing. The sacred grove. Ancient oak trees form a natural circle around a central space, their gnarled branches reaching towards the star-studded sky.

In the center of the clearing stands a massive stone altar, its surface worn smooth by countless centuries of use. Carved into its face is the symbol of our clan—a bear rampant, surrounded by intricate knotwork patterns.

The clan elders await us by the altar, their faces solemn beneath the silvery light of the moon. As we approach, they bow their heads in respect.

"Welcome, Ursa King," the eldest among them intones, his voice carrying clearly across the hushed clearing. "And welcome, future queen. We are honored by your presence on this sacred night."

I incline my head in acknowledgment, feeling Luciana's grip on my hand tighten slightly. "We are honored to stand among our people," I reply, the formal words coming easily to my lips. "May the spirit of the Great Bear guide us on this night of power."

A ripple of approval runs through the gathered

crowd at my words. I lead Luciana to the altar, where we take our places facing our people. The energy in the clearing is electric, a force that seems to vibrate in the air around us.

The head elder steps forward, raising his arms to the sky. "Brothers and sisters," he calls out, his voice ringing with authority, "we gather on this night of the full moon to honor our ancient traditions, to strengthen the bonds of our clan, and to celebrate the wild spirit that lives within us all."

A cheer goes up from the crowd, quickly hushed as the elder continues. "Tonight, we welcome among us one who is not of our blood, but who has been chosen by our king. Luciana Marino, step forward."

I give Luciana's hand a reassuring squeeze before releasing it. She takes a step towards the elder, her head held high despite the nervous energy I can sense radiating from her.

"Luciana Marino," the elder says, his eyes boring into hers, "you have been claimed by our king, branded as his mate. You stand before us now, seeking to truly understand the ways of the Ursa Clan. Do you come here of your own free will, ready to witness our most sacred rites?"

Luciana's voice is clear and strong as she responds, "I do."

The elder nods, a hint of approval in his weathered features. "And do you swear to keep our secrets, to honor our traditions, and to stand by our people in times of both peace and strife?"

"I swear it," Luciana says without hesitation. "By all that I am, I swear to honor the ways of the Ursa Clan."

A murmur of approval ripples through the crowd. The elder turns to me, his expression solemn. "Ursa King, do you vouch for this woman? Do you take responsibility for her actions and her safety on this night of untamed magic?"

I step forward, placing a hand on Luciana's shoulder. "I do," I say, my voice carrying across the clearing. "Luciana is my chosen mate, my future queen. I vouch for her with my life and my crown."

The elder nods, satisfied. "Then let it be known that Luciana Marino stands among us as one of our own. May the Great Bear watch over her and guide her steps."

With that, he turns back to the gathered clan. "Let the ceremony begin!"

A drum begins to beat, its rhythm slow and steady like a heartbeat. Other instruments join in—flutes, strings, and more drums—building a primal melody that resonates in my very bones.

Clan members begin to move, forming a circle around the altar. I guide Luciana to our place in the circle, keeping her close to my side. The music builds, growing faster and more intense with each passing moment.

Suddenly, a roar pierces the night air. Then another, and another, until the entire clearing is filled with the sound. Something deep and primal—the call of the bear that lives within each of us.

I feel the shift begin, the familiar sensation of fur sprouting from my skin, of bones and muscles rearranging themselves. The world around me blurs. In a matter of seconds, the transformation completes. I rise to my full height, my bear form towering over those still in human shape around me. My massive paws dig into the soft earth, and I can feel the raw power coursing through my muscles. The world around me sharpens—scents become more vivid, colors more intense, and every subtle movement in the clearing catches my keen eyes.

All around us, similar transformations are taking place. Where once stood men, now massive bears of various colors and sizes fill the clearing. The music continues, somehow even more intense now that we're in our shifted forms.

I turn my massive head, looking down at Luciana.

Even standing, she barely reaches my chest in this form. I'm worried about how she might react to seeing me—seeing all of us—like this. But the fear I half-expected to see in her eyes is absent. Instead, she looks at me with a mixture of awe and love that makes my heart swell.

Slowly, carefully, I lower my massive head, bringing my muzzle close to her face. Luciana reaches out without hesitation, burying her hands in my thick fur.

"You're beautiful," she whispers, her words meant for my ears alone.

A rumbling purr escapes me, the bear's way of expressing contentment. Around us, other bears are moving, swaying to the rhythm of the music. It's a dance as old as our clan itself, a celebration of our dual nature and the power of the full moon.

As the night wears on, various rituals are performed. Honey and mead are poured over the altar stone, offerings to the spirit of the Great Bear. Young cubs, experiencing their first full moon in shifted form, are presented to the clan elders for blessing. Hunters share tales of great victories, their stories acted out with human speech and ursine gestures.

Through it all, Luciana remains by my side, her presence a steady anchor. I perceive her excitement, her wonder at witnessing these ancient traditions. But I also feel the eyes of the clan on her, watching, assessing.

When the moon reaches its zenith, the head elder calls for silence. The music fades, leaving only the sound of wind through leaves and the heavy breathing of dozens of bears.

"Brothers," the elder intones, his voice carrying easily despite his human form addressing a crowd of bears, "the time has come for the Trial of Instinct."

A ripple of anticipation runs through the gathered clan. This is one of our most sacred and dangerous traditions—a test of control over our wilder nature.

"Who among you will step forward to face the trial?" the elder asks.

For a moment, there's silence. Then, a massive brown bear steps into the center of the clearing. I recognize him as Mikhail, one of our most respected warriors. He's followed by two more volunteers— Pavel, a lithe black bear known for his quick wit, and Dmitri, a younger member of the clan, eager to prove himself.

The elder nods in approval. "Three brave souls step forward. Let the trial begin!"

At his words, several clan members move to the edge of the clearing, returning moments later with three struggling deer. The scent of prey fills the air, causing a stir among the gathered bears. I feel my own muscles tense, the urge to hunt rising within me.

The deer are released into the clearing, their eyes wide with terror as they find themselves surrounded by predators. The rules of the trial are simple—the volunteers must resist the urge to hunt for as long as possible. It's a test of will, of control over our most basic instincts.

Mikhail, Pavel, and Dmitri form a triangle in the center of the clearing, the deer darting frantically between them. The air is thick with tension as we watch, waiting to see who will break first.

Minutes tick by, feeling like hours. I can see the strain on the faces of the volunteers, the way their muscles twitch with the effort of holding themselves back. The deer, sensing the danger but finding no escape, huddle together in the center of the triangle.

Suddenly, Dmitri lets out a roar. In a flash of movement almost too quick to follow, he lunges for the nearest deer. Pavel, his resolve crumbling at the sight of movement, joins the hunt with a growl. Their massive forms converge on the panicked prey.

Mikhail, however, remains steadfast. His massive bear form trembles with the effort of restraint, but he doesn't move from his position. His gaze, brimming with hunger and determination, remains fixed on a faraway spot.

It's over in moments. The deer never stood a chance against two full-grown bears. As Dmitri and Pavel shift back to their human forms, panting and blood-smeared, Mikhail slowly transforms as well, his face etched with exhaustion but pride.

The clan erupts in cheers, with the loudest acclaim reserved for Mikhail's impressive display of control.

The elder steps forward, raising his hands for silence. "The trial is complete," he announces. "Dmitri, you were first to give in to your instincts. There is no shame in this—you held out longer than many twice your age have managed. Pavel, you too showed admirable restraint before succumbing. But Mikhail," the elder's voice swells with pride, "you have once again proven your exceptional strength of will. The clan honors your control and aspires to your level of mastery."

As the elder's words fade, a ripple of energy passes through the clearing. One by one, the massive bear forms begin to shrink and shift, fur receding and paws transforming back into hands. I feel the familiar sensation wash over me as well, my bones and muscles rearranging themselves. The world around me shifts, colors dulling slightly as I return to my human senses. Within moments, the clearing is filled with men once more, myself included, our bare chests glistening with sweat in the moonlight.

I roll my shoulders, adjusting to the sudden absence of my bear's bulk. The cool night air raises goosebumps on my skin, a stark contrast to the warmth of my fur moments ago. As I turn to Luciana, I glimpse fascination and something deeper—desire, perhaps—in her expression as she watches me.

Residual magic pulses through the air, an invisible current that raises the hair on the back of my neck. Around the edges of the clearing, the Ursa women— our clan's witches—stand in silent vigil. Their eyes gleam with an eerie, otherworldly light, reflecting the moon above. Though they cannot shift themselves, their connection to the clan's magic is unmistakable. I can almost see the tendrils of power swirling around them, responding to the primal energy of our transformation.

The cheering dies down, and I feel Luciana stiffen beside me. Following her gaze, I see the reason for her discomfort—several of the unmated males in the clan are watching her with undisguised interest.

A low growl builds in my chest. I may have given Luciana permission to attend the gathering, but that doesn't mean I'm comfortable with other males showing interest in my mate. I shift slightly, positioning myself between Luciana and the rest of the clan.

The elder, sensing the rising tension, claps his hands together. "And now," he calls out, "we come to the final ritual of the night. The Renewal of Bonds!"

At his words, mated pairs throughout the clearing begin to move together. This is perhaps the most intimate part of the full moon gathering—a time for mates to reaffirm their connection under the light of the moon.

I turn to Luciana, seeing the question in her eyes. "We don't have to do this," I say softly, not wanting her to feel pressured.

But Luciana surprises me once again. "I want to," she says, her voice low but firm. "Show me, Gavriil. Show me what it means to be your mate."

Her words send a shiver of wanting through me. Slowly, giving her every opportunity to change her mind, I lean down. My lips brush against her neck, right over the spot where my mating mark lies hidden beneath the high collar of her gown.

Luciana tilts her head, offering better access. The trust implicit in that small gesture nearly undoes me. I feel the familiar tingling in my gums as my fangs descend, a physical manifestation of my bear's presence even in human form. With utmost gentleness, I press my lips to her shoulder. Then, carefully controlling my strength, I graze my elongated canines over the sensitive skin. It's a gesture that echoes my bear's claim—a symbol of dominance and possession, but also of protection and love.

A small gasp escapes Luciana, her hands coming up to tangle in my hair. I can sense the spike of arousal in her scent, feel the way her body trembles against mine. My own hunger rises in response, a low growl rumbling in my chest.

Around us, other couples are engaged in similar displays of affection. The air is thick with pheromones and the sounds of passionate whispers and soft moans. It's a primal, intimate moment—a reminder of the animal nature that lives within us all, even in our human forms.

After what feels like both an eternity and no time at all, I pull back slightly, my hands still holding Luciana close. She looks up at me, her eyes dark with desire and something deeper—a newfound understanding of this part of my nature.

The elder's voice breaks through the haze of lust surrounding us. "The bonds are renewed," he intones.

"May they grow ever stronger with each passing moon."

As if on cue, the first light of dawn starts to paint the eastern sky. The full moon gathering draws to an end.

Slowly, reluctantly, the clan disperses, collecting discarded clothing and making their way back towards their homes. Soon, only a handful of us remain in the clearing—the elders, Sasha and his security team, and Luciana and me.

I immediately pull Luciana into my arms. She comes willingly, pressing herself against me as if trying to shatter any space between us.

"Are you alright?" I ask softly, running a hand through her tousled hair.

Luciana nods against my chest. "I'm... I'm more than alright," she says, her voice filled with wonder. "Gavriil, that was... I don't even have words."

I chuckle, pressing a kiss to the top of her head. "It can be overwhelming, especially the first time. But you did wonderfully, my love. The clan was impressed by your poise."

She pulls back slightly, looking up at me, love and mischief glinting in her eyes. "Does this mean I get to attend all the full moon gatherings from now on?"

I hesitate for a moment, torn between my desire

to share all aspects of my life with her and my instinctive need to protect her. But the memory of how she handled herself tonight, the respect she showed for our traditions, makes the decision for me.

"Yes," I say finally, "if that's what you want. You've proven yourself more than capable of handling our ways."

The smile that lights up Luciana's face is brighter than the rising sun. She stretches up on her toes, pressing a soft kiss to my lips.

"Thank you," she whispers. "For trusting me. For sharing this with me."

I hold her close, breathing in her scent mixed with the lingering aromas of the forest and the gathering. It's a heady combination that makes my head spin.

"Your Majesty," Sasha's voice breaks through our private moment. I look up to see him approaching, respect and urgency etched on his expression. "We should return to the estate."

I nod, reluctantly releasing Luciana from my embrace. "Of course. Lead the way, Sasha."

As we make our way back through the forest, I keep Luciana close to my side. Soft predawn light filters through the trees, casting long shadows across our path. The forest seems different now, as if the magic of the full moon has left a lingering trace in the air.

"What did you think of the Trial of Instinct?" I ask Luciana, curious to hear her perspective.

She's quiet for a moment, considering.

"It was... intense," she says finally. "I could feel the tension in the air, the struggle those bears were going through. It made me realize just how much control you all exert over your animal sides every day."

I nod, pleased by her insight. "It's a constant balance," I explain. "The bear is always there, just beneath the surface. The trial helps remind us of the importance of maintaining that control, especially around humans."

"And the hunting?" she asks, her voice careful. "Is that... normal?"

I can hear the unspoken question in her words—is that what I'm capable of? "It's part of our nature," I say gently. "In that moment, when we give in to our instincts, we are truly wild. But it doesn't define us. We're more than just our animal instincts, Luciana. We're the balance between human and beast."

She nods, seeming to accept this. We walk in companionable silence for a while, the sounds of the waking forest surrounding us.

As we near the edge of the trees, I can see the estate coming into view.

"Gavriil," Luciana says suddenly, stopping in her tracks. I turn to her, concerned by the serious tone in her voice.

"What is it, love?"

She takes a deep breath, as if steeling herself. "I want to thank you. Not just for allowing me to attend tonight, but for everything. For being patient with me as I learn your ways, for trusting me with your secrets. I know it can't be easy, having a human mate."

I cup her face in my hands, marveling at the strength and love I see in her eyes. "Luciana, you are not just 'a human mate'. You are my mate, my equal, my partner in all things. Yes, there are challenges, but they are nothing compared to the joy you bring to my life."

Tears shimmer in her eyes, but she's smiling. "I love you," she says simply. "*All* of you—the man and the bear."

I lean down, capturing her lips in a kiss that pours all my love, all my gratitude into her. When we part, both slightly breathless, I rest my forehead against hers.

"And I adore you," I murmur.

A discreet cough reminds us that we're not alone.

I look up to see Sasha waiting patiently a few feet away, his expression carefully neutral.

"Sorry to interrupt, Your Majesty," he says, "but there are some matters that require your attention."

I nod, stepping back from Luciana. "Of course. What's the situation?"

As Sasha begins to brief me on various post-gathering issues that need addressing, I keep Luciana's hand firmly in mine. The warmth of her touch grounds me, a reminder of why I do all of this—not just for my clan, but for her, for our future together.

The sun has fully risen by the time we make it back to the estate. Clan members bow respectfully as we pass, many offering words of praise for Luciana's conduct during the gathering. I can see the pride and slight embarrassment on her face at their words, and it makes my heart swell with love.

As we enter our private chambers, exhaustion suddenly hits me like a physical force. The energy and emotion of the night catch up all at once, leaving me feeling drained but deeply satisfied.

Somehow sensing my fatigue, without a word, Luciana helps me undress, her touch gentle and soothing. When I'm down to just my trousers, she guides me to the bed.

"Rest, my love," she says softly, pressing a kiss to my forehead. "You've earned it."

I catch her hand as she starts to move away. "Stay with me?" I ask, suddenly not wanting to let her out of my sight.

She smiles, that radiant smile that never fails to take my breath away. "Always," she replies, quickly shedding her clothes and slipping into bed beside me.

I pull her close, her body fitting perfectly against mine. Her scent surrounds me, calming the last lingering traces of my bear's restlessness.

As I drift off to sleep, the last thing I'm aware of is Luciana's steady heartbeat against my chest, a rhythm that seems to echo the words that have become my truth:

My mate. My queen. My everything.

10

THE HEART'S OFFERING

Candlelight flickers across the walls of our private chambers. Outside, the land is blanketed in snow, the winter chill seeping through even the thickest walls. But here, in our sanctuary, warmth surrounds us like a cocoon.

I sit at my desk, pouring over last-minute details for tomorrow's trip to our dacha in Sestroretsk. The wedding is mere months away, and this getaway is meant to be a respite from the whirlwind of preparations. A chance for Luciana and me to reconnect, away from the pressures of clan leadership and royal expectations.

A soft knock at the door pulls me from my thoughts. "Come in," I call, expecting Sasha with some final security reports.

Instead, Luciana enters, a mysterious smile playing at her lips. She's hiding something behind her back, her eyes twinkling with barely contained excitement.

"What are you up to?" I ask, unable to keep the amusement from my voice as I rise to greet her.

Luciana's smile widens. "I have something for you," she says, a hint of nervousness creeping into her tone. "A gift, before we leave for the dacha tomorrow."

Intrigued, I step closer. "A gift? What's the occasion?"

She shakes her head, her golden hair catching the candlelight. "No occasion. Just... because."

With a deep breath, as if steeling herself, Luciana brings her hands forward. In them is an intricately carved wooden box, its surface adorned with symbols I recognize from ancient Ursa lore.

My breath catches in my throat. "Luciana... where did you get this?"

She bites her lip, watching my reaction carefully. "I had it made. With help from Natalya and some of the clan elders. Open it."

With reverent hands, I take the box from her. As I lift the lid, a faint scent of aged wood and metal reaches my nostrils.

Inside, nestled on a bed of deep blue velvet, is a medallion. But not just any medallion. My eyes widen as I recognize the ancient Alexeev family crest, rendered in exquisite detail. The bear rampant, surrounded by symbols of strength and wisdom, all cast in a metal that shimmers with an otherworldly light.

"Is this... star metal?" I whisper, scarcely daring to believe it.

Luciana nods, her eyes shining. "Samara helped me source it. It's infused with protective magic, tied to the Ursa bloodline. The elders... they taught me the ritual to bind it to you."

I'm speechless, overwhelmed by the magnitude of this gift. Star metal is incredibly rare, sacred to our people. And the ritual to bind such an artifact... it's not something easily taught to outsiders.

"Luciana," I breathe, looking up from the medallion to meet her gaze. "This is... I don't know what to say. The time, the effort this must have taken..."

She steps closer, reaching out to touch the medallion. "I wanted to show you... to show everyone... that I understand. That I respect and honor the traditions of the Ursa Clan. That I'm committed to this life, to you, with everything I am."

Emotion wells up in my chest, threatening to

overflow. This woman, this incredible human who has turned my world upside down, continues to amaze me. The thoughtfulness of this gift, the depth of understanding it represents... it's more than I ever could have hoped for.

"Will you..." Luciana's voice is soft, almost shy. "Will you wear it? There's a chain..."

I nod, not trusting my voice. Luciana reaches into the box, pulling out a sturdy chain of the same shimmering metal. With gentle hands, she fastens the medallion around my neck.

As soon as it settles against my chest, I feel a surge of warmth, of power. The metal, despite having been in the cool box, quickly warms against my skin. I can feel a subtle vibration, almost like a heartbeat, pulsing in time with my own. The magic within resonates with mine, creating a harmony that sings through my veins. It's as if a piece of me that I didn't know was missing has finally slotted into place.

"How does it feel?" Luciana asks, her hand resting over the medallion, over my heart.

I cover her hand with my own, marveling at the connection I feel—to her, to my ancestors, to the very essence of what it means to be Ursa. "It feels... right," I say simply. "Like it's always been a part of me."

Luciana's smile is radiant. "The elders said it

would be like that. That the medallion would recognize its rightful bearer."

I shake my head in wonder. "I can't believe you did all this. The planning, the secrecy... how long have you been working on this?"

She shrugs, a hint of mischief in her eyes. "A while. Those 'extra magic lessons' with Samara weren't always about defensive spells, you know."

A chuckle escapes me, tinged with awe. "My dearest love, you always manage to astonish me."

Luciana's expression softens, her hand coming up to cup my cheek. "I meant what I said before, Gavriil. I'm all in. This life, this world... it's not always easy. But it's ours. And I wouldn't have it any other way."

I lean into her touch, overcome with love for this remarkable woman. "Luciana... my queen, my heart... I don't have the words to express what this means to me. What *you* mean to me."

"Then don't use words," she whispers, rising on her toes.

I meet her halfway, capturing her lips in a kiss that speaks volumes. All the love, the gratitude, the awe I feel—I pour it into the kiss, hoping she can feel even a fraction of the emotion swirling within me.

When we part, both slightly breathless, I rest my

forehead against hers. "Dear gods," I murmur. "I'm the luckiest man in the world to have found you."

"I'm the lucky one," Luciana replies, her voice thick with emotion.

We stand there for a long moment, wrapped in each other's arms, the medallion a warm presence between us. It's more than just a gift, I realize. It's a symbol of our bond, of the life we're building together. A physical representation of Luciana's commitment not just to me, but to our people, our way of life.

"You know," I say after a while, a hint of teasing entering my voice, "this sets the bar rather high for wedding gifts. I'm not sure how I'll top this."

Luciana laughs, the sound like music to my ears. "Well, you have a few months to figure it out. I'm sure you'll think of something suitably grand and romantic."

I pull back slightly, raising an eyebrow. "Oh? And what would qualify as 'suitably grand and romantic' in your book?"

She pretends to consider, tapping her chin thoughtfully. "Well, let's see. A star, perhaps? Named after me, of course."

I chuckle, playing along. "A star? Is that all? And

here I was thinking of gifting you an entire constellation."

Luciana's eyes widen in mock surprise. "A whole constellation? My, my, Your Majesty. You do know how to sweep a girl off her feet."

We both dissolve into laughter, the joy of the moment washing away the last of the day's stress.

"Come," I say, taking her hand. "Let's sit by the fire. I want to hear all about how you managed to pull this off right under my nose."

We settle on the plush rug before the hearth, Luciana curled against my side as the fire casts a warm glow over us. As she recounts her adventures in secret meetings and clandestine magic lessons, I find myself marveling at her determination, her willingness to immerse herself in a culture so different from her own.

"… and then Sam nearly set her eyebrows on fire trying to infuse the star metal," Luciana is saying, her hands moving animatedly as she speaks. "I thought for sure you'd smell the smoke and come investigate, but thankfully you were in that strategy meeting with Dima."

I shake my head, chuckling at the mental image. "I can't believe I didn't suspect a thing. You're becoming quite the skilled secret-keeper, my love."

Luciana's expression turns thoughtful. "I wouldn't say that. I don't like keeping things from you, Gavriil. But this... I wanted it to be a surprise. Something special, just for you."

I tighten my arm around her, pressing a kiss to her temple. "It *is* special. More than you know. The medallion itself is a priceless artifact, but the thought, the effort you put into this... that's what truly makes it precious."

She snuggles closer, her hand coming to rest over the pendant. "I'm glad you like it. I was so nervous... I wasn't sure if I was overstepping, or if I'd gotten something wrong in the ritual..."

"You did everything perfectly," I assure her. "The elders wouldn't have helped you if they didn't believe you were worthy. This," I cover her hand with my own, feeling the warm pulse of magic beneath, "is as much a sign of their acceptance as it is of your dedication."

Luciana looks up at me, her eyes shining in the firelight. "Really? I mean, I know some of the clan still have reservations about a human becoming queen..."

I shake my head firmly. "Any reservations they had are fading fast, my love. You've proven yourself time and time again. Your strength, your adaptability, your willingness to learn and embrace our ways... it's more than many thought possible."

With a smile, she conveys both pride and determination. "Good. Because I meant what I said before. I'm committed to this life, to our people. I want to be the best queen I can be, for you and for the clan."

My heart swells with love and pride. "You already are," I murmur, leaning down to capture her lips in a tender kiss.

As we sit there, wrapped in each other's arms before the crackling fire, I'm filled with a sense of profound contentment. Tomorrow, we'll leave for the dacha, for what promises to be a much-needed break from the pressures of clan leadership. But right now, in this moment, I have everything I need right here.

"Thank you," I say softly, breaking the comfortable silence that has fallen between us.

Luciana looks up, a question in her eyes.

"For this," I elaborate, touching the medallion. "For everything. For being you... For being mine."

Her smile is soft, full of love. "Always," she whispers.

The fire burns low, and the night deepens around us. We remain there, talking softly of our hopes for the future, our plans for the upcoming wedding, our dreams for the life we're building together. My heart is brimming with gratitude. For this moment, for this woman, for the life we share. And of hope, for all the moments yet to come…

Little do I know that our time together is far more precious, and far more limited, than I could ever have imagined. But for now, in the quiet of our chambers, surrounded by the warmth of our love, all is right in our world.

Memories continue to flood in, relentless as the rain outside. Our last night together in Saint Petersburg, before we left for our summer estate in Sestroretsk. Luciana's laughter as we made plans for our future. The warmth of her body pressed against mine as we fell asleep by the fire... How could I have known it would be the last time I'd hold her?

The attack at the dacha plays out in my mind, a nightmare I can never escape. The rogue bears under Grisha's command, drawn by Luciana's scent despite my claim on her. The fierce pride I'd felt as she fought valiantly alongside me, proving once again how far she'd come in her training. And then... the moment that shattered my world.

A sob catches in my throat, threatening to break free. I swallow it down, forcing myself back to the present.

I turn away from the window, my reflection a ghostly apparition in the glass. My gaze falls on the liquor cabinet in the corner. The temptation to lose myself in the bottom of a bottle is strong, but I resist. I need a clear head to navigate the mess I've created.

With a heavy sigh, I turn back to my desk. The engagement announcement still lies there, the ink now dry. It represents a future I never wanted, a path I'm now committed to following. But perhaps, in time, it could become something more. Perhaps Cassandra and I could find a way to make this work, to build a partnership, if not a love match.

It's a faint hope, but it's all I have to cling to.

Is this what I've become? A heartless man so focused on duty that he'd force an unwilling woman into marriage?

A low growl rumbles in my throat.

The night wears on. I allow myself one last moment of weakness, and pick up Luciana's photograph, pressing my lips to the cold glass.

"I'm sorry, my love," I whisper. "I hope you can forgive me."

I tuck Luciana's photo away, but her memory

lingers, warm and bittersweet. At once, pleasant moments flood my mind: Luciana's laughter echoing through the halls of our home in Saint Petersburg, her eyes sparkling with mischief as she coaxed me away from my duties for spontaneous adventures. I remember stolen moments in the midst of clan gatherings, her subtle touches grounding me when the weight of leadership felt too heavy to bear.

One memory stands out, vivid and cherished. A quiet evening in Rome, where it all began. The way the setting sun painted the sky in hues of gold and pink, casting a warm glow over Luciana's face as we strolled through Villa Borghese. Her hand in mine, her scent intoxicating, the promise of a future filled with love and happiness stretching out before us.

"Tell me again," she'd said, a teasing lilt to her voice, "how the mighty Ursa King fell for a simple human girl."

I'd pulled her close, pressing a kiss to her forehead. "There was *nothing* simple about you, my love. From the moment I caught your scent, I knew my life would never be the same."

The memory fades, leaving behind an ache so profound it threatens to consume me. But with it comes a resolve, a determination to honor what

Luciana and I shared by remembering the joy, the love, the light she brought into my life.

My hand moves to my chest, fingers wrapping around the familiar shape of the medallion beneath my shirt. Its weight, constant and comforting, grounds me in reality.

I pull the necklace out, the star metal gleaming even in the dim light. The ancient Alexeev family crest stares back at me, a reminder of my duty. But more than that, it also symbolizes Luciana's love, her acceptance of my world, her dedication to our life together.

Luciana may be gone, but our story, our love, is forever branded in my memory. Etched into my very soul, as permanent and unbreakable as the star metal around my neck.

Our time together, our love story that began in the eternal city, will always be a part of me. And as I face the challenges ahead, I'll carry it with me—a secret strength, a hidden light in the darkness of duty.

As I turn back to the engagement announcement on my desk, I make a silent vow. For Luciana, for the love we shared, I will endure. I will lead. And I will never, *ever*... forget.

ABOUT THE AUTHOR

Silvana G. Sánchez is the USA TODAY bestselling author of sinfully addictive dark fantasy new adult novels *Ash and Snow, Steel and Stone, Written in Blood,* and more paranormal and fantasy romance stories, including the *Vesely Academy* series. She lives in Mexico with her husband, son, and two adorable Shih-Tzus she calls her dragons. When not plotting away in her writing den, she's known to poke eyes in her practice as an ophthalmologist.

For more information:
silvanagsanchez.com
sgs.author@gmail.com

www.ingramcontent.com/pod-product-compliance
Lightning Source LLC
Chambersburg PA
CBHW051228210726
48290CB00003B/854